Teacher

Erotica

C J Edwards

Adult Reading Material
All characters depicted are over the age of eighteen.
British spelling used throughout.

ISBN: 9781718053366

DEDICATION

With thanks to

Francessca's PR & Design

Kelsey Burns

CONTENTS

SUB TEACHER

I knew Russell wasn't revising and I was going to catch him at it. My fourteen year old son had an aversion to hard work. While my husband watched the boxing, I snuck upstairs and pressed my ear against his door. It sounded like he had the telly on and I listened hard… to the sound of sex!

"What the hell!" I burst in and caught my boy fumbling with himself at his desk and the image of a naked white woman and black man on the screen.

"Mum!"

"Don't you Mum me, you disgusting boy!" I feigned a horrified expression. "You're supposed to be doing algebra and instead, you're doing God knows what while watching hard core porn!"

"It's soft porn," Russell bleated.

"It looks hard to me," I yelled, watching the man fondle the pretty young woman on the computer screen. "How do you even know the…!" I stopped short, I recognised the girl in the film!

"Who is this?" I insisted. "And where did you get the film?"

Russell only half answered. "I just downloaded it off a site a mate gave me and …"

I finished it for him. "And it's your substitute form teacher!"

He adopted his sheepish expression. "Yes!"

"Has anyone else seen this video?"

"Not as far as I know."

"Get on with your maths!" I took his laptop downstairs and handed it to Johnny. "Look what I caught your boy with," I said with a wry smile.

"A chip off the old block," he laughed, watching the film run. "Quality porn!"

"Never mind that. Do you recognise the slut?"

Johnny almost squinted at the screen for a minute. "Fucking hell," he finally exclaimed. "It's not that cute little teacher is it?"

"Yes it is," I smirked. "And it's parents evening next week. Shall we both go?"

"Let's get the last appointment shall we?" Johnny was now making a tent in his pants.

We were clearly on the same page as usual and the least I could do was relieve his discomfort. "Come and give me a good shafting and I'll tell you what I've got in mind for the naughty little minx!"

I considered myself a very sexual woman and my Johnny was a good fucker. As he rooted me so well, my mind ran wild with thoughts of Corrie Willoughby and what I was going to do with her. I was only submissive with my husband and that was simply because he liked it. By nature, I was a Domme and I loved sex with woman just as much as with men. Corrie may have had worked in the adult industry but I was quite sure I was going to open her eyes and I was equally convinced she was going to accept my advances. That was, if she wanted to remain a teacher! "Fuck me harder," I encouraged my man. "Imagine I'm the little teacher."

"You'll need punishing then," Johnny grunted, pulling out of me and effortlessly flipping my petite body over. As his big cock widened my tender arsehole, I moaned like the hussy I was. Corrie was going to squirm like a jellied eel when my husband fucked her.

*

The parents evening was only four days away but it seemed to take forever. I phoned the school and said we would be late and confirmed we would be able to discuss matters in private with Russell's form teacher. The school secretary assured me the interview would happen in Miss Willoughby's classroom and we wouldn't be disturbed. *Perfect!*

That brief conversation alone left me uncontrollably hot. Despite it being the middle of the afternoon, I crept up to my bedroom, peeled off my damp knickers and frigged myself stupid. Looking up at the mirrored ceiling of our bedroom, a gorgeous thirty eight year old milf looked back at me. Honey blonde hair, lithe body and a good rack, she was one hot mother! As I pushed my flowered skirt up to my waist and began with small circles around my clit, my mind wandered with an image of what Miss Willoughby would look like helpless beneath me as I plundered her hot little box. Lost in the fantasy, I practically ripped my blouse and bra off to expose my perky tits and I mauled them hungrily with one hand as I battered my pussy with the other.

Johnny didn't know what had hit him when he got in from work that evening; I practically raped him. Pushing him back on his favourite armchair and pulling his fly down, I rode him for a good half an hour and countless orgasms, until his legendary self-control finally lost to my tight body and he sprayed my insides like a fireman damping down a raging house fire.

Thursday finally came round and I took all afternoon choosing my outfit, bathing and waxing my intimate bits. By the time Johnny got in, I'd wanked myself stupid as well. All I could think about was that innocent looking young woman and what we were going to do with her. I had wondered for days what that 'porn film' was all about and how experienced she really was. Maybe she really was an experienced slut who would gladly open her legs or perhaps it had been a one off student thing that she deeply regretted and she was in fact as innocent as she looked. I was inclined to think the latter, but we would see. The film was actually pretty soft. I had watched it a least a dozen times; usually with a finger in my slot and could see the sex was actually simulated. She was with another man; also well-endowed and another woman; acting out a frenetic pussy lapping session that gave me a lady boner. If she was really a lesbo virgin, she wouldn't be for long. And I loved to break a virgin!

Walking the school corridors at seven o'clock was odd. The last few parents were leaving and I guessed the other teachers had mostly left as well as the car park was virtually deserted. I noted that Miss Willoughby's classroom door was blacked out and when we knocked and entered, I also saw she had left her key in the inside lock of the door. *Perfect!*

"Mr and Mrs Arnold?" The pretty young redhead looked up and flashed us a dazzling smile with perfect teeth. I took a moment to fully appraise her. I had only seen her in passing before and that was mostly when she was swaddled in a playground coat. Now we were up close, I was very impressed. Her face was a perfect almond shape with green eyes and slightly chubby cheeks that made her look almost angelic. Her body was mostly hidden by her desk but it couldn't disguise her impressive pair of baps in a peasant blouse. This was a very attractive woman in her prime and she would have the confidence to go with it. She was going to need to be broken quickly.

"It's Corrie isn't it." I didn't phrase it as a question and enjoyed the look of confusion the use of her christian name caused the inexperienced teacher. She indicated the school desks in front of her and looked mildly shocked when we both perched on the edge of the desks, rather than sitting down like students on the chairs. "How's our naughty boy getting on then?"

Johnny and I listened avidly as the young woman described our boy as positively as she could. I only interrupted once to catch her off guard again. "You're a substitute, aren't you Corrie?"

"Well, we're normally called supply teachers," she smiled again. "But yes. I'm doing maternity cover, although..." She suddenly stopped when she realised she'd opened a door on her own personal life that was unnecessary.

I had that effect on other women. "I prefer sub but go on honey," I coaxed her.

She had no choice. "The Head has just offered me a full time contract from September."

"That's great darling," I smiled. "Is that your first proper job?"

The smile was beginning to fade. "It's my first permanent teaching contract, yes!"

I exchanged a quick glance with my husband that didn't go unnoticed and then let her continue with her appraisal of our son. Not surprisingly he wasn't setting the world alight with his academic abilities and was picking up regular detentions for cracking jokes at his teachers' expense. I wasn't concerned. I knew he was doing well.

After ten minutes of teacher monologue, I decided it was time to up the ante a little. "Would you like to see what he was doing for homework last night, Miss Willoughby?" I asked sweetly, pulling my iPad out of my big handbag.

"Of course," she answered, having no idea what she was letting herself in for. I turned it on, pressed my finger to the screen to activate it and pressed play on the waiting video, setting the tablet in front of the unsuspecting teacher.

"What the heck is this?" She tried to bluff her case but her wavering voice and nervous eyes betrayed her.

"Good try Corrie," I smiled. "Keep watching!" The film ran through her blow job, lesbian scene and then a pretty convincing few minutes of her being taken doggy by the big black man. Her pretty face just dropped further and further as the film played. I enjoyed her discomfort. I took another glance at my husband, who was stifling a smile. "What would the head teacher say if he knew you were a porn star?" I asked innocently.

"It's not porn," she answered. "It's all simulated and it was a one off. I was a broke student and got offered some modelling work…"

"It looks real to me," I shook my head. "What do you think, darling?"

"Oh, very real," Johnny agreed. "I mean, look at her face. There's no doubt she's taking that black cock!"

"It was acting!" Corrie snapped back, now very nervous. She sensed the dynamic had changed and had no idea what to do about it.

"Well, I'm not sure," I said. "Let's ask the Head!"

"Christ no!" Corrie couldn't control herself. "Please don't," she added in a contrite voice; her big green eyes beginning to fill with tears.

"I'm guessing you would lose your job if the Head found out about these?" Corrie nodded her head in reply to my question. I looked across to Johnny again. We were a good double act. "What do you think Honey?"

"Well we can't just let it go," he reply slowly. "I mean, she needs to be punished!"

"P-punished," Corrie stammered. Her eyes grew larger as Johnny walked across the door, locked it and put the key in the pocket of his jeans.

"That's right," I told her. "Punished! You should understand the concept, being a teacher and all!" I was now stood in front of the trembling young woman. I took her hand and drew her to her feet, so we were facing each other. Her eyes were almost at the same level as my tits, she was so short.

"What are you going to do to me?" Her voice trembled as she spoke and I was pleased at the question. As an experienced Domme, I realised straight away that the clever girl had already made the mental step of seeing herself in our hands.

"You'll see," I said, beginning to unbutton her blouse. "All you need to do is what you're told and things will be just fine."

Things were moving fast and Corrie couldn't cope with it. "Please don't," she begged and her hands shot up to grab mine.

Johnny was ready though and already standing behind her. He seized her firmly by the upper arms and drew them down to her sides. His overwhelming strength sent the right message and the young teacher stopped struggling. Instead she stood passively as I removed first her blouse and then her modest cotton bra.

"Oh my fucking God!" I was genuinely impressed. "You've got to see these tits, Johnny. They are perfect!"

Hubby turned the girl around by the shoulders and ogled her. "Better in the flesh, darling," he smiled. "There's just one thing that would make them perfect." He cupped one in his hand and idly tweaked the nipple with his thumb as Corrie began to blush bright pink.

"Go on then!" I knew my husband well and had a good idea what was coming next.

"My spunk of course! Splattered all over the little slut and dripping off her nips!"

"I'm not a slut," the young teacher stammered.

I turned her back towards me. "If you're not yet, Sweetie. You will be when we're done with you." I dipped my head down to her luscious tits and to her utmost horror, I sucked one of those perky nipples into my mouth.

It was lucky Johnny still had a tight hold of her because Corrie started to struggle again. "No! I'm not a dyke, stop it!" The words were forceful but not backed up by the soft and meek tone of her voice.

I enjoyed the sensation of having a perfect but unwilling tit in my mouth. Rolling my tongue around the tip engendered an instant reaction. She was clearly very sensitive there. I tucked that information away for use later.

I reluctantly let the nipple drop from my mouth and pulled up one of the hard plastic chairs. "This is supposed to be a punishment," I snapped in a mock strict voice. "Bring her here," I told my husband. He helped me bend her over my thighs, with her palms flat on the floor. I flicked her skirt up to her waist and rested my hand on her firm bum cheek.

She went without struggling but I pinned her firmly to me with my spare arm. Her naked tits hung along the outside of my thigh and gave me a tingle in my fuckbox. "Are you ready for your spanking, naughty girl?" I goaded her as my hand continued to wander.

"You've got to be fucking joking," the normally demure young woman yelled and then her tone changed. "No! Don't do that!" She started to panic as she felt her knickers come down.

It took me a while to wrestle the tiny panties down to the teacher's knees, while holding her in place with the other. I was stronger than I looked but Johnny was only an arm's reach away; standing, looking at Corrie's snatch with a big smile on his face. I ran a manicured finger down her slit. "Mmmm! Look how gooey she is already, darling!"

"She's gagging for it," Johnny agreed. "Do I get to fuck her yet?"

While the helpless young woman struggled to get her head around that statement, I brought my palm down hard on her right buttock cheek.

"Arrrgh!" It wasn't too loud and she did her best to muffle it but it was unmistakably a scream of pain.

"You better bite your lip girl," I warned her. "If we're interrupted, you'll be explaining to the head why we're punishing you!"

My next blow left a big pink mark on the other cheek. Corrie tried harder to hold her cry in this time but it was still too loud. I looked up at Johnny. "The silly bitch is gonna need gagging!"

My horny hubby didn't need any persuading. Walking around to her head, unzipping as he went, he had his cock in his hand before she saw what was happening. Gripping a handful of hair on the top of her head, he tugged upwards painfully. Her mouth opened in a cry and he just shoved his hefty slab of meat straight into her throat.

I guess Corrie had never been deep throated as she made a heck of a fuss; gagging, retching and wriggling. But that was fine as it was all muffled. I started a regularly drumbeat of slaps on her rump; turning the whole area bright red.

By the time I needed to rest my sore palm, Johnny was humping the girl's face like a hungry cunt. Strange slurping noises came from the back of Corrie's throat and mixed with the rhythmic slapping sounds of my man's rock hard lower abs hitting her forehead. I reached under her chin and between Johnny's hairy thighs to gently squeeze his balls. He was close, I could tell, so I gave the teacher's hot little pussy a rub.

I knew all too well how much Johnny could ejaculate but the boy surpassed himself. A choking flood of spunk, snot and tears flowed down her throat as he pumped his muck into her belly. However it may have looked though, she seemed to enjoy it. Her jerking continued as he pulled out and with a long cry, she filled my hand with her honey.

I let Corrie fall to the floor in a quivering heap and picked up her blouse. "Tidy yourself up, girl," I ordered her. "You're coming back to ours for the night." She didn't say a word but let me help her to her feet and pulled on her top; not even noticing she no longer wore her bra or knickers.

*

Our house was only a fifteen minute drive away. I drove her car around the corner and parked it in a big supermarket car park before getting into the back of our BMW with her. I then spent the journey idly playing with her pussy as she rested her head on my shoulder and closed her eyes.

We had of course arranged for Russell to be away for the night so the house was empty when we got there. I had taken a bit of time to get our big bedroom ready for our guest. First of all though, I stripped her completely in the middle of the lounge and pushed her to her knees. "You've sucked my husband off," I told her. "Now it's my turn."

"Please no, Mrs Arnold," she begged. "I don't like women! Not in that way!"

It really made me wet to hear the gorgeous young teacher call me by my married name when naked and on her knees. I couldn't wait any longer. "Shut up cunt," I snapped and mashed her face into my trouser crotch.

Rubbing my cotton covered cunt into her face just made me more frustrated. I pushed her away and frantically stripped off my bottom layers, grabbing her by the hair and hauling her with me as I collapsed back into an armchair. "Now lick me, you dumb bitch, or I'll whip the skin off your tits."

There was only a little hesitation. Once she had taken the first couple of tentative licks, Corrie apparently decided she quite liked the taste, as she set to it with gusto. And she was really good! I closed my eyes and enjoyed the enthusiastic lapping of my brand new girlfriend.

I was losing myself into a semi-orgasmic dream state when I realised the licking had stopped and Corrie's pretty face was rubbing up and down my sloppy vent. I opened my eyes and looked straight into my husband's beautiful eyes as he smashed his cock into the pretty teacher. "How is she?" It seemed the obvious question to ask.

"Very tight!" Johnny was gripping her tight buttocks hard enough to leave bruises as he forced his XL cock into her XS pussy.

Corrie lifted her head and I could see her eyes were dreamy, like a junkie. "Please don't cum in me," she moaned quietly. "I'm not on the pill!"

I laughed and grabbed a big handful of her hair, to push the pretty face back into my cunt. "If my Johnny wants to knock you up, that's exactly what he'll do, silly bitch!" I looked over her back and winked at my husband. "I bet she's got an even tighter hole though!"

Johnny loved to bugger a reluctant young woman; the more petite the better. And I loved to watch! He carried on humping her until she was close to the edge and the pulled out. While I was holding her face into my lady garden, I saw him subtly change his position… and push!

Corrie's head flicked up and she screamed. Really screamed – not like the half-hearted affair she let rip while being spanked. "Aaaaaaarrgh!" It sounded like she was being ripped apart.

"Tight?" I teased my husband, as I held Corrie in place.

The exertion was clear on Johnny's face; veins popping out all over. "Fuck! You have no idea! I'm not even a quarter of the way in!"

"Wanna take her upstairs? We need to get it on film remember!"

"Why not!" Johnny gave the girl's arse a good slap as he pulled out and pulled her to her feet.

Corrie's pretty face was a picture. Glistening with my juices on her nose and around her mouth, she displayed a complete confusion of emotions as she struggled to cope with what was happening to her. "What do you mean, film?" The question was muttered almost as an afterthought as Johnny threw her over his muscular shoulder and started upstairs.

""We're going to make a much better porno than the other one," I laughed. "Sub teacher 2!"

"I can't," she complained.

"You *will*," I snapped. "If you behave yourself, we'll keep it in our private collection."

"Behave myself? What does that mean?"

We had arrived at our huge bedroom and Johnny dumped her unceremoniously on the bed, "You'll see!"

We had two HD cameras set at either side of the room and we had them wired into our telly on a split screen. We were going to capture the action at both ends and I didn't want to miss a moment of the delicious little expressions that would be displayed across Corrie's pretty face. When she saw the way the room was set up, those expressions started playing. Her bright eyes flashed around and focused on the leather pommel horse, Sybian and the chains hanging from the ceiling and her mouth dropped open.

"You're going to learn a few things tonight, little subbie," I informed her, picking up a long leather sleeve. I started to buckle it up her arms; pinning them behind her back and she began to struggle once she realised her supposed freedom was about to be taken from her. "Take over here," I asked my hubby and moved around the bed. He pulled her up on to her knees and *whack!* I slapped her hard across the face.

As Corrie swayed on her knees and her eyes teared up, I gripped her nipples hard and squeezed. "You've got some obedience to learn, my slut," I barked and literally pulled her off the bed by her tender nubs. I took her straight over to the leather horse and pushed her backwards; landing her precariously on her back, with her arms trapped beneath her and her toes on the floor. I grabbed a thick leather belt and fastened it around her middle to hold her firmly in place. "Cane, crop or tails?" That question was for Johnny.

He smiled his big, jovial grin. "Well, she is a teacher. It'd be churlish not to cane her!"

My smile matched his own. I knew what that cane felt like on the arse and it was by far the most painful of the three options. The idea of her big, flawless tits being striped with the flexible bamboo gave me an instant lady boner. It definitely required a gag!

"This one?" Johnny nodded his approval. The penis gag could have been modelled on his own knob. It was big and fat. I held her nose for a couple of seconds and shoved in in her open mouth; watching her expression turn from fear to distress as the tip lodged against the back of her throat and activated her gag reflex.

Swish! I started her caning without any more delay. The gag successfully muffled her screams to all but a faint cry but her reaction was telegraphed by her red face, wide teary eyes and her legs, which came straight off the floor and oddly flopped open in a *fuck me* pose as they had nowhere else to go.

Johnny was only too happy to oblige. He grabbed her hips to hold her steady and sank his pork sword in the girl; straight up to the hilt as I continued her lashing.

Corrie's tits soon became a crisscross of livid red stripes as the tears rain freely down her rosy cheeks and her upper body jerked in protest. Her lower body seemed to have other ideas and her hips were already making little humping motions to meet my stud's hammer blows. I couldn't help but stripe her toned, virginal belly as well and then stepped back to view my artwork. Johnny took advantage and leant over to suck on those sore looking nips, speeding up his humping and showing all the signs of coming soon.

"Go on darling," I coaxed him. "Fill her full of jizz!" Those words energised my man but seemed to have the same effect on Corrie. I pulled the gag off to hear her expletives as her body bounced around. "Oh fuck, yes! Yes! Yeeees!" Corrie came, just as Johnny filled her womb with his healthy sperm.

As Johnny pulled out, I pushed my muff on to her face as I reached down to pull her legs up to put her knees by her ears. "You didn't give her a buggering," I admonished my husband. "Do you want me to do it?"

"Why not? You're not bad as a botty bandit," Johnny laughed.

"Open her up for me then," I smiled. He pushed some of his spunk towards her tightest hole and rubbed a finger around her rosebud; making her moan into my box. I accepted a few surprisingly effective licks from my slut and then disengaged, leaving Johnny to finger fuck her reluctant arsehole, while I found my favourite lump of latex.

It was a double-ended dildo but not the run of the mill type. Her end was long and fairly thick; although a lot slimmer than Johnny. My end on the other hand was stubby, wide and tapered. It was basically a handle for my rock hard pussy muscles to hold on to. I'd had many a sloppy cunt with this but a tight, virgin bottom was new territory for me. I was going to be working hard for my prize.

"How's she looking?" I looked across myself to see Corrie's legs had dropped and she was struggling once again as Johnny fucked her arse with two fingers. *When was the girl going to learn?* "Lie still!" My strident voice silenced the room and Corrie fell still.

"That's good," Johnny grinned. "She just loosened right up and I'm up to my knuckles!"

"Don't loosen her too much," I cried in mock despair. "Hold her legs!" Johnny pulled her feet right up by her head again. I gave the dildo a run of my special KB-W lube and spread her buttocks apart with the palms of my hands.

Corrie's pretty little starfish winked at me, as I opened her cheeks as wide as I could. I placed the tip of my false cock right on the centre of it and gave a little flex of my hips to lodge it inside.

"Uh!" That first little moan from Corrie as I started to open her arse was encouraging and very horny. I pushed a little further and hit some serious resistance so I stopped for a moment and gave her anxious clit a bit of attention; circling my thumb lightly around the hood and watching the bean emerge like a tortoise from its shell.

"This is going to hurt, honey," I warned her. "But you're used to pain now, so be a big girl!" I put my hands back on her buttocks and pulled apart as Johnny placed his big palms back on her tits. I braced myself and nodded to him.

Johnny pulled hard on the girl's nipples and I hammered my hips forward. I felt a tremendous resistance but ploughed on with all my strength; which was considerable. And after what seemed an eternity but was probably less than two seconds, her ring muscle collapsed and I was deep inside the sweet girl.

Corrie screamed like a stuck pig as I ravished her and then just sobbed as I started to slowly bugger her. Johnny now had his sack on her face and Corrie was obediently licking the salty skin as I took her. I let her lick for a moment and then spoke to my husband. "Step back Honey, I want to see her face. You can whip her tits again if you want," I offered as a sweetener.

Not surprisingly, Johnny took me up on that. He chose a multi-tailed whip with soft leather tails. That would warm her up a lot, I knew. He didn't hit her hard and she responded well. I could see her face now and saw an enchanting mix of pain and pleasure. She was moving in the right direction.

Things then moved fast. I saw her expression change markedly all of a sudden and I upped my pace. "How's your little butthole, Corrie," I teased and she just moaned in reply. Johnny backed off again and I bent over to kiss her.

"Oh God!" She moaned into my mouth and kissed me back passionately. I grinned inwardly. "Want to cum, baby cakes?" I squeezed her hot tits and began to smash my cock into her little shitter.

"Oh fuck! Oh fuck! Oh fuck! Yeeeeees!" Corrie's arsehole convulsed and her whole body flipped about under the tight belt. She was coming big style.

That was good but I wasn't quite off yet. I pulled out a little fast and made her yelp. I pulled off the belt, lifted her off, frantically pulled off the arm sleeve and pushed her towards the bed. "Get on your back and spread your legs," I ordered.

I practically leapt on top of her, mashed my cunt into her face and started to lick the remainder of Johnny's sperm from her slot. "Oh Christ," I moaned. I couldn't remember ever feeling so horny before.

Our coupling was right under one of the cameras and Johnny picked up the other to get some great close ups of Corrie's face and pussy. When I came, I was accompanied by another powerful eruption from our slut and my pleasure was total. I screamed and shivered for several long minutes and then collapsed on top of my lover; completely sated.

Corrie was now ours and she clearly knew it but I told her anyway. "We'll send you a copy of the edited video. Would you like it to go to your school account or a personal one?"

"No. My Gmail account would be fine thanks, if that's okay."

I smiled at Johnny. "You're our little sub now Corrie," I told her. "You're ours whenever we want you. Do you understand?"

She looked a mess, covered in spunk and pussy juice and was still trapped underneath me. "Yes," she said quietly.

"Yes, what?"

"Yes, Miss!"

TAKING ADVANTAGE OF TEACHER
(HYPNOSIS SEX #2)

Chloe Richards looked at herself in the full length mirror in her bedroom. She liked what she saw. Her big, heavy breasts with their fried egg areola and long nipples showed no real sign of droop, her stomach was still flat and her hips were womanly but not wide. She felt alive and very sensual and thought about what had happened over the previous twenty four hours.

She knew she had had sex with one of her students. *No wait, two of her students – there was Melanie too!* Of course she knew that was wrong but she couldn't feel guilty about it. She also didn't know why she'd done it. The whole business didn't make sense to her and the more she thought about it, she realised there were big gaps in her memory. She cupped her tits in her hands and squeezed; she was very horny. Lying back on her bed she thought about the upcoming party and her fingers wandered down between her legs.

Edward was a very happy young man. All those years of science geekery had finally paid off when he perfected his hypnosis machine and successfully tested it on his biology teacher, Miss Richards; and fucked her. Tonight was going to be the mother of all parties. He had invited six of his mates around. Well six other boys anyway; he didn't really have any mates. They were sure to turn up because they knew that ten of the best looking girls had also been invited. They didn't know that the girls were going to be there thirty minutes earlier, with Miss Richards, and had an appointment with Edward's machine. It was going to be a hell of a party!

Chloe stood nervously outside the front door to Edward's parents' house. She was still not sure why she was there but she had told the girls she would be and had asked them to turn up. As she self-consciously smoothed her dress down over her stomach, she thought she could hear them giggling in the distance. Taking a deep breath she rang the bell.

The door opened almost immediately and geeky Edward stood there leering at her. Immediately and inexplicably, she felt damp between the legs as his eyes roamed freely over her big tits and the rest of her hour glass figure. Once she was inside, he hurriedly closed the door and thrust his tongue down her throat. She had no resistance; she wanted him too.

"What would you like to drink?" the young man asked politely, when he had finished groping her.

"Do you have vodka and tonic?"

"Of course," he laughed and led the way into the kitchen.

Edward had no sooner given Chloe her drink when the doorbell rang again. It was the girls.

Chloe went to answer it at Edward's request and was confronted by the group of excitable eighteen year olds, all wearing too much make up and very little clothing. "Hello Miss Richards," they all sang in chorus. "What are you doing here already?" Michelle added in a playful tone.

"Come on in girls," Chloe replied. "There's something I need to show you before the party starts."

This was the key element to the evening that Edward had programmed into the unsuspecting Chloe's brain with his hypnosis machine. She led the girls into a room at the back of the house that was set up like a cinema, with the machine at the front, looking just like a television set. Edward was waiting for them. "Have a seat ladies," he announced. "I want your opinion on my invention before you start drinking all the free booze!"

The girls all looked at each other with amused expressions but sat down all the same. Edward asked them to all look at the screen and the moment he was sure they all had, he flicked the switch.

All of a sudden, the room was bathed in a pale white light and the chattering stopped as though Edward had switched that off at the same time as clicking the machine on. Eleven women sat transfixed as they looked into the light box and their minds were rewired.

Watching the time tick over on his watch as he stood behind the device, Edward looked at the sea of pretty faces and thought about which of the girls he was going to enjoy. He had already broken Melanie in of course but there were several others of the girls who were just as gorgeous: Hannah with her fluffy chestnut hair and big tits; Georgina, the cheeky slim blonde; Gail the class swot, short and delicate. Before any of them though, he was going to get another blowjob from his teacher. She was just so good at it! Switching off, he spoke to them all. "Okay girls, we're here to have a party and that means having a good time. Anyone who doesn't have sex tonight is boring." He paused. That suggestion should be enough to ensure ten pairs of knickers would be coming down shortly. "There's plenty of booze in the kitchen," he added. "Go and help yourself." As the girls got up and moved out of the room in a daze, he stopped Chloe with a hand on her arm. "Not you Miss Richards," he said. "I want you to come upstairs with me."

Chloe's head was still spinning as she followed Edward up the stairs. She knew he was going to have her again and it was wrong but it didn't even occur to her to refuse. When she entered the bedroom, she had to gasp. It was clearly a teenage boy's den; with model planes and tanks still in evidence but it was also an electronics lab. There was an entire wall filled with monitors and a workbench below, covered in wires, modules and half built computer things. Edward led her into the middle of the floor and clumsily groped and kissed her again, before reaching behind her to unzip her dress and let it drop to the floor. Pushing his small hands into her bra, Edward squeezed the vibrant flesh and pulled on her long, fat nipples. She began to moan with desire, leaning her forehead on his shoulder as he fondled her. Her bra went next and then Chloe felt the boy's hands on her shoulders; pushing her to her knees. She went willingly and found herself looking up at his burgeoning crotch.

Chloe knew what she wanted and unzipped his fly without being told. Reaching inside, she pulled out the thick, long prick he concealed so well and began to slowly rub it. Leaning forward, she placed a kiss on the end and then opened up to engulf the silky shaft in her warm, moist mouth. Bobbing her head back and forward in time with her hand, Chloe felt very turned on and couldn't help letting her hand drift down to her damp panty gusset.

Edward's hands came up to grip her soft hair and gently guide the backwards and forwards motions that were giving him some much pleasure. Sucking his flesh hard, Chloe caught a salty taste of pre-cum and knew from past experience it wouldn't be long before he blasted her throat with spunk.

There was noise on the landing and Chloe assumed the boys had arrived. And then, without warning, the door flew open and she found herself looking up at a very large and very angry looking man. "What the fuck is going on?" blustered Edward's stepdad, a man Chloe had met several times before and feared for his quick temper and physical power. Chloe let the cock fall from her lips and looked up at him, suddenly feeling very vulnerable. She saw recognition flash in his eyes before he turned back to his stepson, who still stood with his cock hanging out and was clearly terrified. "I said, what the fuck is going on," he repeated and cuffed Edward around the head for emphasis.

"I'm just having a bit of a party," Edward whined. "You said that you and Mum would be away tonight."

The huge man turned back to Chloe. "I know you, don't I?" he said, narrowing his eyes. "You're his fucking science teacher!" He seemed to think about things for a couple of seconds and then reached down to grab the woman by the arm and yank her to her feet. "You! Go back to the party," he barked at Edward. "You can come with me," he said to Chloe in an equally harsh tone.

As he dragged her along the landing, the stepdad, who Chloe remembered was called Pete, lectured her on her shortcomings. "...having sex with one of your students will mean you'll never work again as a teacher and probably get locked up too," he went on. The helpless woman knew he was laying the ground work to blackmail her into having sex with him. What he didn't realise was it was all completely unnecessary. She knew full well she would submit to whatever he wanted. Moments later she was in the master bedroom, waiting in the middle of the floor for the inevitable. Pete was fiddling around in a bedside drawer, pulling things out, and then he was behind her. Pulling her arms together, he snapped a leather strap around her wrists and secured them tightly together, before pushing her roughly back on to her knees. "Now you'll see how a man likes his cock sucked," he growled.

Grabbing a good handful of hair, he yanked Chloe's head back so her mouth opened in a cry and took the opportunity to push his cock straight in. Rather than stopping in her mouth though, he went all the way into her soft throat; making her gag.

When her air supply suddenly stopped and she gagged loudly with the unaccustomed intrusion in her gullet, she expected Pete to withdraw. Far from it though! He held her head securely in place and kept his meaty cock lodged in her throat. "That's it slut," he muttered. "Get used to the feel of that and we'll get on just fine." Just as Chloe thought she would pass out due to lack of oxygen, he withdrew to allow her a breath and then rammed back in again to start a steady rhythm. He had complete control of the helpless woman with his cock in her throat and as he battered his way in and out of her throat, her entire body moved in sympathy. Reaching down to squeeze and fondle her big naked breasts, he gave her the first compliment of the night. "You are one well-stacked woman Miss Richards, what the fuck you see in that scrawny step-son of mine is anyone's guess."

Pete lasted a hell of a lot longer than Edward ever did but when he came, it was volcanic! Chloe's first warning was his hands tightening each side of her head, to the extent he actually started to hurt her. Then his pace quickened and he began to dance around, before his cock started to twitch in her mouth. Finally the explosion happened. The first load went straight down her throat and it was all Chloe could do to not retch. Another twitch of the cock and her mouth was full and then he pulled free to spray some more all over the teacher's pretty face.

When the brutish man released her, Chloe slid to the floor but she wasn't there for long. Grabbing her by the hair and bound wrists, Pete pulled her over to the bed, sat on the edge and draped her over his knee.

"Clearly you have to be punished for seducing one of your students," he laughed, "and it looks like it'll have to be me who does it." Grabbing her panties in one big hand, he wrenched them off with a loud ripping noise and started to paddle her upturned arse.

"Arrrgh! Arrrgh! Arrrrrgh!" Chloe couldn't contain herself as the blows rained down on her big round bottom. It hurt like hell but the utter humiliation of being spanked as a mature woman was far worse. Pete stopped after about ten smacks and caressed her tender arse with his rough hand. She took a few deep breaths to recover and realised she was panting like a dog. His hand wandered down to her waiting pussy lips and stroked them with a surprising degree of tenderness. Her moans turned decidedly erotic. "Oooooooh!"

Once he had the horny teacher on the brink of orgasm, Pete started his spanking again. This time though, the smacks were a little less harsh and the intervals longer, the pauses being filled by meaningful caresses of her arse, pussy and then her tight little bum hole. The blows still hurt but somehow they were good. Chloe's sex throbbed and she wriggled her hips to try and rub her cunt against her tormentor's leg. She knew what she wanted and that want was becoming desperate. "Please fuck me," she said quietly.

Pete stopped smacking for a moment. "What was that?" he asked.

"Just fuck me will you," Chloe repeated at normal volume. "Please fuck me!"

Pete laughed and stood up, holding the helpless woman by the hair so she didn't hit the floor. Pushing her backwards, the back of her thighs hit the bed and without arms free to support herself, she fell flat on her back on the bed, with her legs in the air. Laughing again, he unzipped himself, grabbed the young woman by her ankles and pulled her bodily towards himself, before draping her legs over his shoulders. Carefully placing his fully revived erection against her moist hole, he leant forward and penetrated her in one movement.

Chloe lay back as the brute of a man seized her sensitive breasts in his hands and rocked his pelvis to fuck her hard and fast. As her pleasure began to rise through her vibrant body once more, she tried to figure out why she had submitted to this powerful man so readily. She didn't like him; that was for sure. But she was definitely attracted to him in a big way. She felt every inch of his thick, knobbly cock as it reamed its way through her moist intimate flesh and his fingers played a symphony in her nipples. Before she knew it, a tsunami of feelings washed over her and she came with a scream. "Oh Christ, yes, ooooh!"

As she shuddered and cried, Pete withdrew and effortlessly flipped her on to her front. Her pussy was still pulsing as he entered her arse, gripping and parting her round buttocks as he dug for dirt. This was mind-blowing. It hurt, *Christ it hurt!* But it was an ecstatically good pain. As he humped her hard and fast, Chloe opened her eyes for a moment and locked gaze with a pair of wide open blue eyes. Petite, shy Gail was in the doorway. Screwing up her eyes again, she rode her orgasm all the way back up to the top as the fat cock coughed and spat a load of scalding spunk into her colon.

Of course Pete had seen Gail too. "Have you ever had anal, little one?" he asked as he withdrew from Chloe. A shake of the head was all he got in response. Holding out his hand, he drew the college girl to him, kissed her and then persuaded her to her knees. The hypnosis machine seemed to be having the desired effect on all the young women. All the same, Chloe didn't need to see the brutal slaughter that was bound to follow; her sense of maternal concern may have been placed on hold by the machine but there were limits. Gathering her things together, she left the room, closed the door behind her and dressed on the landing, before making her way towards the stairs.

As she passed Edward's room, Chloe heard a very girly giggle and couldn't help but investigate. Edward was leaning over his bed, where Vanessa and another of the girls were locked in a sixty nine. She couldn't be sure but she thought it was Susan. Vanessa was rubbing Edward's long cock with one hand as she fondled the other girl with the other. Edward heard the door open and looked up. "Ah, Miss Edwards," he exclaimed. Vanessa looked up at her teacher's name and then shrugged and continued licked her pal's pussy. Edward tried to concentrate on Chloe for a moment. "The girls all need a bit of a nudge to start fucking," he muttered. "They're probably all still stood around the kitchen table," he added. "Go and tell them what to do!"

Chloe took that as a command and walked downstairs. Sure enough, the party had moved to the kitchen and looked like any other teenage party, with awkward conversation and a bit of fumbling. She moved straight in to achieve her mission. Singling out Mandy, a shy dark hair girl with big eyes, she smiled at her and whispered in her ear. "Which one do you fancy the most?"

"Definitely Mark," Mandy replied without hesitation.

"Why don't you give him a blow job then?" Chloe teased. "Boys love that you know!"

Mandy walked across the kitchen to Mark; a rugged boy with matching hair and to Chloe's surprise, she squatted down in front of him. Rather than taking him somewhere quiet, she took her teacher's suggestion as a literal command: unzipping him, she pulled out his cock and popped it straight into her mouth.

The rest of the room stood agog as shy little Mandy started to bob her head up and down and no-one was more surprised than Mark. Not that he made any attempt to stop her! As they all watched with their mouths open, Chloe moved around the room to Sally. "Wouldn't you like Eric and Haydn to spit-roast you?" she asked innocently as though talking about shoes or something. Sally walked over and took both boys by the hand and disappeared into another room. Chloe then paired up all of the other boys with willing girls until she was left with Georgina and Melanie. Chloe found her mouth watering as she looked at the naive Melanie and remembered her first lesbian experience with her the previous week. "You two had better come with me," she sighed and led them back upstairs.

Ten minutes later, her face was covered in Georgina's nectar as Melanie sucked and licked her teacher to a shattering orgasm. As she came, Chloe Richards reflected on how her life had fundamentally changed. She had no idea how or why, but she was very content.

A LESSON FROM TEACHER
Teacher Sex #1

Parents evenings were a pain in the arse at the best of times, thought Sarah Hadrian to herself as she tidied her classroom. To have to prolong the agony an extra day to suit one parent made it even worse. Still, she needed to see Josh Smith's mum, he had some serious behavioural issues and she was very apologetic about being unable to get away from work the previous day.

Sarah had been a teacher for as long as she could remember. Now just the wrong side of forty, she was nevertheless a very attractive woman. Her long dirty blonde hair framed a very pretty face and her statuesque body kept her greedy fiancé very happy. That kept Sarah happy too, but only to a point. She was very bisexual and needed some female love from time to time. It had been over a year since her sub, Mary had moved away and she was hungry again. Oh and Sarah was very dominant. She always took the lead in her relationships; to a greater or lesser degree.

The classroom door opening jolted Miss Hadrian out of her daydream. She looked up to see a sheepish young woman standing in the doorway. Stacie Smith was a bottle blonde in her early twenties and got Sarah's attention straight away. She was some six inches shorter than her own five foot nine with a lovely, curvy body. She dressed like a slapper, miniskirt, heels and crop top but all the same, she had the body to pull it off. And the thing Sarah liked best of all was she was clearly submissive. Her downturned eyes and nervous body language told the experienced Mistress everything she needed to know.

"Miss Hadrian?"

"Yes, hello Mrs Smith, please come in," answered Sarah.

"It's Miss Smith," replied the young mother boldly and stepped up to the teacher's desk. Launching straight into a pre-prepared script she then started to berate Sarah for telling her boy off, not helping enough with his maths and God knows what else, before Sarah interrupted her.

"Why don't you take a seat, Miss Smith," she said sharply, indicating one of the child-sized chairs and tables in front of her desk.

Stacie struggled on to the little chair, unsuccessfully trying to stop her skirt riding up her thighs. Looking up at the teacher behind her big desk, she suddenly felt like she were in school herself and closed her mouth, ready to be told what to do.

Sarah let the silence hang for a few moments before speaking in slow measured tones. "Josh's behaviour in class is not acceptable, Stacie. May I call you Stacie?" She didn't expect or need a reply and just continued on. Six year old boys need lines drawn at home and need to be pulled up sharply when they step over them. Who is the disciplinarian at home, you or Josh's father?"

Stacie stuttered for a moment before finding her words. "Josh's dad doesn't live with us," she mumbled.

"Well that answers the question then," snapped Sarah. "You clearly don't administer discipline, do you? You don't know the meaning of the word." Stacie looked like a rabbit in the headlights. All the colour had drained out of her face and her pretty mouth hung open. Sarah continued. "Josh walks all over you at home, doesn't he Stacie?"

Suddenly the young Mum burst into tears. "Yes," she sobbed. "I don't know what to do with him."

Sarah looked at the hysterical woman for a while as the tears rolled down her face and her make-up ran. Four and a half minutes, she mused. That had to be a record. Slowly rising from her desk, she walked around and pulled the girl to her feet; taking her into her arms. Gently embracing her as she blubbed, she stroked the peroxide hair and shushed her.

As she calmed down, Sarah leaned back a little and took her pretty little face in her hand to raise it to her own. "I'm going to teach you all about discipline, Stacie, if you want me to. Is that okay?"

The tall teacher felt Stacie's soft tits heaving just below her own as the cogs turned behind her eyes. Getting no reply, she repeated herself in a sterner town. "I said, is that okay, Stacie?"

Stacie nodded her head, not at all sure about what she was agreeing to. Sarah released her and walked across the classroom to look the door. She didn't want the caretaker blundering into what she had planned next. Walking back, she took Stacie's hand and led her into the story area; a big alcove with another desk for her and a big soft carpet for the children to sit on. "Stand there," she commanded, sitting back behind the desk.

"Discipline for adults is a little different to that for children," she began. "The principles are the same though. There can only be one person in charge and that person is me. Do you understand?"

"Yes," said Stacie meekly and lowered her eyes.

"Yes what?"

"Yes Miss."

"That's better," said Sarah. "Now, are you ready to do exactly what I tell you?"

"Yes Miss."

"Good. We're going to start with a number of exercises to test your obedience. Make no mistake. If you disobey me, you will be punished."

Sarah let that information sink in for a moment before continuing. "Right," she said sharply. "Remove your top and skirt."

Stacie looked like she'd been punched in the guts. "But, I can't," she stammered.

"You can and you will, young lady," Sarah snapped. "Now remove your top and skirt now or I will do it for you. We have complete privacy here, no one can disturb us."

With trembling hands, the young mother pulled her crop top over her head and unfastened the button on her denim skirt, letting it drop to the floor. She stood there in patterned bra and panties, the sort of thing a teenager would wear. A red flush spreading from her face and across her chest as she felt the stern teacher's eyes all over her.

Sarah assessed her young student carefully. She had already broken her and the delicious young woman was hers for the taking but she still had to take things carefully and keep her under control or at this early stage she could lose her. Her eyes roamed over the exposed flesh. Her tits must have been at least a D cup and looked very firm. Stacie had a substantial bra on but didn't look as though she really needed it. Her stomach was flat and flared out to what could definitely be called child bearing hips. Her cotton panties were stretched tightly over a very prominent mound and the hungry teacher couldn't wait to see what was hidden. She knew she would not have to wait much longer.

Getting up from her desk, Sarah took her big handbag with her and walked behind the young MILF. She could feel Stacie's nervousness as she vanished behind her and knew she was dying to turn round but didn't dare. Reaching in to her bag, she pulled out a pair of handcuffs and commanded her to put her arms behind her back to secure them in place. She then reached into her bag took out a pair of surgical scissors, before turning the young woman to face her.

Looking Stacie in the eyes, Sarah slowly and meticulously snipped her bra straps and let the cups drop away to reveal a set of very perky breasts. "You are absolutely gorgeous, Stacie," she said and gently stroked the soft skin around her nipples. Stacie bit her lip and moaned, not really knowing how to react. Have you ever made love to another woman? Sarah asked, bending her neck to suck one of the young woman's juicy nipples into her mouth.

"No," mumbled the MILF. "I'm not a lesbian."

Sally laughed, the nipple still in her mouth. "I'm not either; I can assure you I am very fond of cock." She paused to suck hard and sent a shiver down Stacie's back before continuing. "That doesn't stop me appreciating women though when an exceptional one comes along. And believe me, Stacie," she said, running her finger tips over the young woman's panty-clad clitoris and almost making her knees buckle. "Believe me when I say, you are exceptional."

Stacie was in conflict. She had never even contemplated having sex with another woman and yet here she was, allowing her son's teacher to molest her. Miss Hadrian was sucking hard on her nipple now and now her fingers lightly traced a path down her stomach and slipped inside her knickers. "Ooooh!" She couldn't hold the loud moan back as the teacher began to massage her clitoris.

Sarah pushed the yummy mummy up against her desk and pushed two fingers deep into her pussy. Stacie was lost in the throes of passion now. Her head was thrown back and she was uttering obscenities. "Oh fuck, you bitch. Fuck me like that you cunt, oh come on…!" The teacher made a mental note of that language. She would need to be punished for that later. In the meantime she fucked her hard with her fingers, feeding greedily on her juicy tits from time to time.

Stacie was on the verge of orgasm when Sarah suddenly stopped and removed her fingers. She opened her eyes and began to beg. "Don't stop now. Please, do me some more!"

Sarah bent forward and kissed the young woman on her full lips. "I'm sorry sweetheart but you're going to have to wait. You're coming home with me and if you're a good girl, I'll let you come as much as you want."

"I can't come home with you," Stacie mumbled as Sarah unfastened the handcuffs. "I've got to pick Josh up from my mom's!"

"Phone her now," said Sarah in her no-nonsense voice. "Tell her you have an emergency of some description and she needs to keep him overnight."

Stacie pulled off the remains of her bra and pulled her crop top on over her head. The bra went into the bin. She dug her bright pink phone out of her handbag and steeled herself to call her mother.

The call lasted a good ten minutes and Sarah tidied her classroom while she waited. Granny was clearly not happy by the end of it. Nonetheless, Stacie had freedom overnight. She finished getting dressed and let the teacher lead her out of the classroom and towards the car park. Reaching in to her handbag to fetch her keys, Sarah stopped her with a hand on her arm. "No. you're riding with me. Your car will be fine in the car park." She didn't want the young mother having second thoughts and driving herself home. She had Stacie in her control and that's where she was staying.

She drove home with Stacie sat next to her. They made small talk and Sarah deliberately didn't give her any clues about her domestic arrangements. She was certainly in for a few surprises that evening and by the time she had finished with her, she would be a changed woman.

They pulled into Sarah's driveway and the teacher could see the younger woman's eyes almost popping out of her head at the size of the house. The cogs were turning and no doubt she was wondering how a primary school teacher could afford to live in such luxury. She didn't know about Craig of course. She would be meeting him later but not just yet. Sarah had texted her lover and asked him to stay out of the way for now.

They entered through the kitchen and Sarah made her guest a quick gin and tonic. Stacie started to refuse it but a stern look told her to just shut up and drink it. She left her in the kitchen for a few minutes while she went to prepare a few things and by time she was back the tall glass was empty. "I don't normally drink gin," said Stacie, already a little tipsy.

Sarah led the young woman into her big lounge and stood her in the middle of the floor while she sat down in an armchair. "Right then, young lady," she said. "It's time for you to learn a few things. Are you ready?" Stacie nodded. "Right," Sarah continued. "You will only speak when spoken to and when you are addressed you are to reply. You are only to address me as Mistress, Miss or Miss Hadrian and you are never to use bad language in my presence. Do you understand?"

"Yes Miss Hadrian," came the reply. Stacie was brighter than she appeared.

"Good. Now undress for me and do it slowly," said Sarah. "Imagine you're a stripper."

Stacie swayed her hips from side to side and ran her hands up and down her body. She wanted to make herself as alluring as possible for this curious woman but still didn't really know why she was doing this. She didn't like being told what to do and she definitely did not have sex with other women. It's just that somehow, this felt right. She slowly lifted her crop top over her head and pushed her skirt down to the floor.

"Good girl," said Sarah, when the young woman was standing in front of her completely naked. "Come over here!"

Stacie took the few steps across the lounge towards her Mistress and stood completely still with her face reddening as the older woman began to play with her pussy again. Her head began to

42

swim and she was vaguely aware of being spoken to gain. She quickly snapped out of her daydream to focus on the words. "I have to punish you now, my pet," she said. "You remember what happened in the classroom don't you?"

Stacie would never forget what happened in the classroom as long as she lived but she wasn't sure what the teacher was referring to. "Er, yes Miss," she mumbled.

"I am referring to your bad language," Sarah snapped. "Now, bend over my knee."

Stacie couldn't believe she was being treated like a naughty little girl. Nonetheless, she couldn't stop herself doing as she was told. She arranged herself over the older woman's thighs, her hands and feet braced on the floor. The teacher's rough woollen skirt chafed against her naked skin and her nipples felt rock hard. The first blow, when it came, really hurt and as her right hand swung back to cover her bruised flesh, she yelled out at the top of her voice, "Awww!"

"You will remove that hand right now, young lady," said Sarah. "That is your only warning. Next time I will double the number. You are free to make as much noise as you wish but remember what I said about bad language."

Stacie put both hands back on the floor and Sarah continued the spanking. She was careful not to hit too hard for this first time but quickly turned the lovely round buttocks a glowing red. Stacie had the perfect bottom for spanking. She was fleshy without being fat and it meant her bottom moved in a delightful way with each smack.

When her bottom was an even red all over and Stacie was openly sobbing, Sarah called a halt to her punishment, dropping the young woman on to the floor. "That is the most mild of the punishments you will receive from me if you refuse to behave," she said in her sternest voice. "Now, are you ready to show me what a good girl you can be?"

Stacie looked up sheepishly. "Yes Miss Hadrian," she replied meekly.

"Good. Take my knickers off for me."

Stacie went into her rabbit in the headlights routine again.

"I said take my knickers off. Do not make me repeat myself again!"

"Yes Miss Hadrian," said the younger woman sheepishly and nervously reached under the teacher's long skirt. Not believing what she was doing, Stacie began to work the flimsy material down the teacher's long legs and over her feet.

Sarah lay back in the armchair, pulled the skirt up to her waist and spread her legs wide. "Do you like my pussy, Stacie," she asked in a soft voice.

Stacie had been avoiding looking at it but now having no choice, she stared at the pretty waxed area between Sarah's legs. She was completely smooth and very attractive there. It looked like the lady garden of a much younger woman; everything was nice and tight and her clitty was hidden away in its little hood.

"Make me cum, my little girl," Sarah purred.

Stacie gingerly reached over to touch another woman for the first time. It felt soft and moist under her fingers and was almost like touching herself. She moved her finger tips around Sarah's clitoris and was surprised to see it pop out straight away. Rubbing it gently got an immediately reaction from the teacher, she started to moan and shuffle around.

Feeling the yummy mummy's fingers on her cunt was too much for the horny older woman. Reaching down, she grabbed a handful of soft hair and pulled Stacie's face into her pussy. "Lick me, you little slut," she moaned.

Face to face with a woman's private parts for the first time, Stacie was all at once nervous, worried and very aroused. She took a deep breath in and her nose was all at once full of Sarah's very heady scent. Her head started to spin and she felt lost in the moment. Leaning forward a little, she put out her little tongue and swiped it along the pink lips, not really knowing what to expect.

Sarah was so horny she thought she was going to burst. Pulling Stacie's little face right into her sloppy pussy, she rubbed her slimy juices all over her, trying to hump herself to orgasm. To her delight, she felt a little tongue pushing inside her and start to lap the fluids out. Spurred on, her hips began to dance on their own accord as she used the submissive woman like a dildo, humping her face relentlessly.

Stacie could hardly breathe with her mouth and nose crushed into the teacher's soaking wet pussy. Pulling her face away a fraction to grab a breath, she replaced her tongue with a finger, pushing it deep inside and curling around where she imagined the g spot was. That was enough it seemed to push Sarah over the edge.

"Oh shit!" Sarah yelled at the top of her voice. Her hips humped like mad and she wiped endless slimy cum all over her pet's pretty face. Coming down eventually, she pulled Stacie up to kiss her on her soiled face and to give her a loving cuddle.

"Well done, little one," Sarah purred. "That'll keep me going for a little while so now I can focus on doing you properly." She got up and pulled a pair of handcuffs and a blindfold out of a drawer, quickly putting them on the naked woman. "That's you ready for a visit to the playroom."

Stacie felt herself being led by the wrists across the lounge and down the hall. She paused for a moment while Sarah unlocked a door and then she was gingerly walking down some stairs, with her Mistress holding her tightly to guide her. She was led through another door and heard fluorescent lights coming on before her blindfold was removed.

"Welcome to the playroom," Sarah announced.

Stacie looked around the big room and was completely knocked out. She was clearly in the cellar and by the size, it must run completely under the house. At first glance it was set out like a gym and indeed there was some gym equipment in one corner; a treadmill for instance. The great majority of the items however, were not the sort of thing you would find in a high street gym: The room was dominated by a huge crucifixion cross at one side, with straps that were clearly designed for restraint. There were ropes and straps hanging from the ceiling at various points, benches and what looked like vaulting horses but smaller. There were racks and racks of whips, crops, harnesses and goodness knows what else and there were machines and things that she could only guess at their purpose and there was the biggest bed Stacie had seen in her life.

"I can see you're impressed," chuckled Sarah. "It cost us a small fortune to build all this. Fortunately, we have a big fortune," she joked. "Now then, where shall we start with you?" Pulling her across to where a rope hung from the ceiling, Sarah clipped the handcuffs into it and pulled the rope up through a pulley. Stepping back to look at her prize, she was impressed. Stacie's body was stretched as tight as a bowstring as she just managed to keep her toes on the floor. Her body was as lean as it could be and her already very perky tits were drawn up so the nipples pointed to the ceiling. She ran her hand slowly down the length of the young woman's body, enjoying feeling her tremble beneath her fingers.

Stepping back, Sarah enjoyed the sight of her beautiful young slave, displayed to her best. She was clearly nervous and her breath was a little ragged. All the same though, the lust was visible in her eyes. Closing the gap again, Sarah began to explore the succulent body. She kissed and sucked on Stacie's cheery red nipples while fondling her moist pussy. Moving behind her, she stroked the flawless skin on her back before pulling her still pink buttocks apart to reveal a pretty brown starfish. She pushed her tongue inside and rimmed the young woman for a few moments, making her squirm around and complain.

Sarah moistened a finger and inserted it in the helpless girl's bottom. "Am I right in assuming you are virgin back here?" she asked.

Knowing better than to lie or prevaricate, Stacie answered immediately. "Yes Miss. I've never done anal. I think it's dirty."

Sarah laughed. "It is dirty, chicken. That's one of the things that makes it so naughty. But there are ways to make it a little cleaner." Sarah removed her finger and patted the young woman on her tender bottom, making her jump. "Well you won't be a virgin by time you leave. My boyfriend likes nothing better than breaking in pretty little things with tight arses."

Stacie wanted to speak out but knew she would only be punished and she was in such a vulnerable position she had no guts at all. She hadn't agreed to have sex of any sort with a man, let alone her first anal. But then, she didn't really agree to her first sex with a woman either. She said nothing but watched as the teacher walked across to a cabinet and took out a small cock-like object and a tube.

"You're much too tight at the moment," said Sarah, squeezing lube onto the butt plug. "Even if Craig manages to get his huge slab of man meat in you, it's going to hurt like hell. This will help loosen you up a little. She was behind the young woman now and Stacie jumped again as lube was squirted straight into her back passage. "Now, try to relax and push back a little," she said in a low voice, encouraging Stacie to push her bum out with her fingers in her pussy.

Stacie felt the tip of the plug at her anus and it felt strange and unnatural. Then she felt pressure building up as Sarah pushed, before it popped through and entered her properly. The whole feeling was odd, like she had been invaded. The walls of arse were being gently stretched, which felt a little uncomfortable but not really painful. Sarah pushed the plug all the way in and her sphincter closed around it to hold it firmly in place.

"That's nice and snug," said Sarah. "Now, while your bum is being opened up a little, I think it's time you were properly fucked!" Releasing her pet from the pulley, she led her over to the bed and laid her on her back, exchanging the handcuffs for leather cuffs that were attached to the headboard.

Her captive secure again, Sarah undressed for the first time. Stacie watched carefully as the older woman removed her clothes, revealing an outstanding body. Her natural honey blonde hair flowed over slim shoulders and down to a very pert pair of firm tits. The rest of her body was long, slim and firm. As she moved, muscles rippled under her skin. Sarah was in very good shape for her age and she knew it. She turned around to get something out of the cabinet again before facing her young sex slave with a harness strapped around her waist and two big dildos in her hands.

"I'm going to tell you know exactly what's going to happen to you," she said. "First of all, I'm going to eat you out until you cum.

And then, I going to make a decision on which of these bad boys, I'm going to fuck you with. This one," she held up an eight inch cock with a wide girth, "or this one," she held up the other one which was at least ten inches long but a little slimmer. "When I've finished fucking you, I may have your virgin arse or I may leave it for Craig. I haven't decided yet."

Placing the dildos down next to the tube of lube, Sarah bent over and hungrily snogged the younger woman, pushing her tongue right into her mouth as she roughly fondled her tits. Sucking the long nipples right into her mouth, the teacher noted the little whimpers from Stacie with a great deal of pleasure. Working her way down the flat belly, she gently pulled the little pussy lips apart with her fingers and pushed her tongue right inside the hot little passageway.

"Oooooh!" Stacie couldn't contain her pleasure as she was licked out for the first time in a very long while. Unable to do anything but lie there and take the pleasure, she thrashed her head from side to side and started to babble as Sarah brought her off with long licks that went all the way from her arsehole to her clit.

It took no time at all for the young woman to cum and Sarah had to hold her down with all her strength to finish her off; her hips jerked so violently. Licking her lips, she stood up and bet over the bed to kiss Stacie's soft lips again. "I've decided on long and slim," she said with a smile.

It took the Mistress less than ten seconds to snap the dildo into place in the harness and rub lube all over it. Without any delay, she picked up the young woman's legs and held them in the crooks of her strong arms as she fed the mushroom end into her tight pussy and then impaled her with a big thrust.

Stacie went wild. This was a big phallus for her at the best of times but the butt plug had made her feel even tighter. She began to make horny little screams from the back of her throat, which encouraged Sarah to fuck her even harder. "Ah! Ah! Ah!"

Little Stacie was pushed up the bed with each thrust, to be pulled back into place by the friction of her tight twat, wrapped around the dildo like a rubber band. She leant over to suck those juicy nipples once again, encouraging the screams from Stacie to increase in volume and pitch. A crescendo of noise began to build; the slapping of flesh as she hammered into the pussy mixed with Stacie's vocalisations until suddenly she came with a cry. That wasn't going to stop Sarah though. She just continued to ride the girl through her orgasm and kept the fanny battering going until the hapless girl had cum again and again.

Eventually Sarah collapsed on top of the exhausted young woman. Kissing her tenderly as she lay there with ten inches of rubber still wedged inside her, she stroked her soft hair. "My lover's going to be here to have you in less than an hour," she whispered. "We'd better get you ready!"

Stacie just gave a satisfied sigh.

SEDUCED BY TEACHER

"Just a moment young lady," Miss Duncan called out sharply and Emma froze in her tracks. *Busted!*

The statuesque English teacher marched up the deserted corridor and quickly caught up with the teenager. She was a good foot taller than the petite blonde and towered over her. "I think you owe me an explanation!"

Emma knew exactly what she meant but didn't really know what to say. She had sat on the front row during her detention and spent the entire hour lusting after her teacher. And that wouldn't have been quite so bad if she hadn't been so obvious. Her nipples had been so rock hard that they must have been very visible through her school blouse, her chest rose and fell with her heavy breathing and sweat ran off her brow despite the cool air conditioning. Worst of all, she handed in a blank sheet of paper in lieu of a two-hundred-word essay.

Amy Duncan was no fool and she understood young women far better than they understood themselves. The girl clearly had a crush on her. The only question was whether she was going to take advantage of it. She looked down at Emma's big blue eyes and clear skin, her slender body with its big tits, pushing against a white shirt that looked to be a size too small and her tight little bottom. The girl was screaming out for a good fucking and Amy's own highly sexed body was responding to her. She lifted Emma's chin with a long middle finger and fixed her with a hard stare. "Well?"

Emma visibly crumbled. "I...but...you...!"

Amy made up her mind. "You fancy me don't you?"

Emma opened and closed her mouth without a sound and then blushed a bright pink.

Amy's finger now lightly traced a path along the girl's cheek. "I know you Emma," she told her. "I've seen girls like you come and go for years." Her finger now moved down the girl's neck. "Some of them I ignore," she continued. "Some of them I tease," her finger was now at the girl's cleavage. "And some of them I take," she seized Emma's juicy breasts in her hands. "And I fuck them silly." She bent her head to kiss the whimpering girl on her full lips. "Would you like me to fuck you, little Emma?"

"Yes Miss," the girl whimpered softly.

It was almost six o'clock in the evening and the school was virtually deserted. All the same, Amy was taking a big chance in fucking with the eighteen-year-old sixth former in the corridor.

However, she couldn't help fondling her there for a few minutes. The risk of getting caught and its implications sent a tingling of excitement straight to her hungry pussy. She tore open the girl's blouse and roughly pulled her bra cups down to expose cherry pink nipples to her lips. Emma's skirt was pulled up to her waist and the teacher quickly explored the girl's sweaty little quim. The teenager's pussy was soaking wet.

Less than five minutes later, Amy released the girl and stepped back to look at her. "You look like you've been raped, little slut," she chuckled. And sure enough, as the teenager lent back against the wall with her heaving tits exposed and her skirt round her waist, that's exactly what she looked like. "Make yourself decent," the teacher told her. "You're coming home with me!"

The teacher walked the corridors to the car park with Emma in tow. She pushed open the double door to the outside and enjoyed the feeling of the early evening sun on her face as she turned towards her Mini Cooper.

"Ah, Miss Duncan." A man's voice hailed her from across the car park.

Amy whipped her head around to see Mr Shepherd, the Deputy Head and less than a second later she glanced down at Emma to see whether any evidence of her ravishing was showing. The girl had pulled her torn blouse together and tied it under her bosom in a non-regulation but relatively decent fashion.

Mr Shepherd looked Emma slowly up and down, clearly enjoying the view. "You're in school rather late aren't you, Miss Morris?"

Amy answered for her. "She's been in detention Mr Shepherd, for her, erm, wardrobe malfunction."

Mr Shepherd's eyes had settled on Emma's big, firm tits. "So I see," he salivated.

"Well she's not catching the bus like this," Amy said as she hustled Emma past the dirty old man, "so I'm taking her home." Without waiting for a reply, she pushed the girl into the passenger seat of her Mini, jumped into the driving seat and sped away from the school.

"You told him, the old perv," Emma started.

"Get your tits back out," Amy snapped.

"Buuut!" The teenager stuttered.

"Shut up and show me your tits", the teacher said coldly, reaching across to pull at the loop below the girl's perky breasts. A quick tug and they bounced back out again. Amy reached across with her left hand and tugged on the girl's nipple. "I'm going to fuck your silly little brains out slut," she said. "What do you think about that?"

Emma thought a lot about that. At eighteen, she was very much still a virgin as, despite being drop dead gorgeous, she just couldn't seem to communicate with the boys at school. She had never considered herself attracted to girls but she was certainly now reconsidering her sexuality. This woman was driving her crazy. "I think I'm going to cum if you keep doing that Miss," Emma gasped.

"You're going to be cumming all evening," Amy told her as she pulled into the parking space outside her block of flats.

Once they were through the front door, Emma expected Miss Duncan to be all over her but instead, she turned her back on her and walked to the fridge to get a bottle of beer. She then walked into her lounge without so much as looking at her student, clearly expecting her to follow. Emma hesitated for just a moment and then followed on.

Entering the lounge, Emma saw her teacher sat on an upright wooden chair in the middle of the carpet. Still fully dressed in her silk blouse and long skirt, she sat up with perfect posture; accentuating her bosom and flat stomach. "Undress for me," she said. "Slowly!" Emma's hands came up automatically to the loop under her breasts again.

Amy flicked on some slow music and Emma's hips began to move to it. Her school shirt hung open and she eased it down her arms to reveal her pretty pink bra. Then her regulation skirt was unzipped and shrugged downwards to leave her standing just in her pretty pink lingerie. "What a dream," Amy sighed as she ogled the young woman. Her big tits stood proud on her slim chest and her panty gusset was stretched tightly over an interesting looking mound. "Let's see the goodies then," she nodded.

The bra went first and Amy caught her breath at seeing those beauties in all their glory. When the girl's hairy blonde muff was revealed, it was all the school ma'am could do to resist the urge to rape her student there and then. "Come here," she commanded firmly. Emma walked across the room and couldn't help making her slim hips sway in a way that made the older woman's mouth water. She stopped at her teacher's knees and looked up expectantly. Amy grabbed her by the arm and forced the teen down and over her knee, shuffling her around until she was satisfied with her position; feet planted on the floor and hands on the other side, her head and tits hanging downwards. "That's better," she said. "You're now in a perfect position for continuing your punishment." She began to fondle Emma's firm buttocks; squeezing the flesh and letting her fingers gently explore the dark crease between them. "Have you ever had a man here?" Her fingertips lightly brushed the girl's puckered little rosebud. Emma shook her head violently. "Oh," said Amy, suddenly inspired. "Well, in that case. What... about… here?" Her finger suddenly ran between Emma's taut labia and the edgy teen almost jumped out of her skin.

"I've never had anyone there either," Emma confessed.

She stopped dead. "You're shitting me. Do you mean to say you're a…?"

"Yes. I'm a virgin."

Amy seemed to get very excited at that confession. Her hand began to fondle Emma's pussy. "You won't be for much longer," she told her protégée. One more stroke and then her hand came back. "First of all though, you need to be punished for not working in detention." She slapped her firmly across the left buttock, *craaack!* The firm flesh wobbled and immediately started to turn pink.

Once she had started, Amy began a steady fusillade of blows on the girl's unprotected rump. "Arrrgh! Arrgh! Arrgh!" It really was a punishment. She couldn't remember the last time she suffered so much pain and discomfort as the bright pinkness spread quickly across her rear.

"When was the last time you had a spanking, little girl?" Amy asked as her hand continued to punish. "Did Daddy used to smack you when you were naughty?"

Emma's mind went straight back to her last spanking from her big, strong Daddy. She had been caught smoking at school and he was so disappointed with her. The emotion of that day six years before; guilt and a sense of hopelessness came flooding back to her. She felt very, very sad. And then something different. Not only was her arse stinging like hell but her pussy was very, very moist.

Just when she felt she couldn't stand it anymore, Emma felt a sudden relief as the spanking stopped. Amy's long fingers moved to her pussy again and slipped easily inside, exploring the entry and then probing deeper. "A virgin eh?" The teacher purred. "What are we going to do about that?" Emma didn't reply; there seemed no need. Amy shifted her legs and let the student drop on to her own knees. Her hand, now freed, went behind her to rub her tender bottom. She felt a firm hand on the back of her head push her face towards her teacher's groin. "Now show me how much you want me, little one," Amy whispered.

Emma was in unknown territory but seemed instinctively to know what to do. Her nostrils filled with the heady smell of her teacher and that seemed to make every molecule of her body tingle. Gently pushing Amy's long skirt up her slender thighs, she eventually found her lingerie. Silky, fragrant French knickers. *Crotchless French knickers!* She gently parted the opening and was surprised to find the mature woman was completely bald. Slipping her tongue between the folds of silk, she tasted Miss Duncan for the first time and was pleasantly surprised. A little tangy, sour but slightly sweet. She liked it!

Amy was now very horny and not in a mood for patience. Pushing the girl's face right into her minge, she urged her on to suck and lick. Emma tried to keep up with the demands of her Mistress but pretty soon she was just providing a face for Miss Duncan to get off on. She kept her tongue out and Amy just ground her moist flesh against it and her nose, her chin and in fact every angle of the girl's face. Emma just concentrated on breathing.

"Oh fuck! Oh fuck! Oh my fucking God, yes!" When Amy came, there was no mistaking it. Emma found her face crushed against the woman's cunny for a full minute as she leaked copious streams of juice into her mouth. When she was finally released, she collapsed on to the floor, gasping.

Amy recovered fast. "Would you like some of that sweetie," she asked the girl, still in a crumpled heap on the floor.

"Oh yes Miss," Emma gasped. Amy took her hand and pulled her effortlessly to her feet; leading her along the hall. She pushed a door open and bundled the girl through. Emma then found herself in the master bedroom and what a bedroom it was. She had once heard someone say that a woman's bedroom is a reflection of the woman and when she looked around; she suspected that was exactly the case here. The décor was a deep red, edged in black and the bed was an enormous four poster. There was a bench of some sort in front of it and a table with a large selection of wicked looking whips and such like. It didn't look like the sort of place you relax and Emma wondered if Miss Duncan really slept there. Guided up on to the bed, she lay back and instinctively spread her legs as her Mistress climbed up between them and began to blow on her pussy.

The next twenty or thirty minutes were undoubtedly the most intense of Emma's young life. Amy played her body like a virtuoso pianist; taking her up and down the stairway of pleasure but never quite letting her orgasm break over her. The older woman was literally driving her crazy. Finally, Amy lifted her head. "Would you like to come now Emma?" she asked simply.

"Oh God yes!"

"Say please!"

"Christ! Please. Please make me cum."

Amy flicked her long tongue across Emma's very erect clitoris and made her shiver. "You'll have to do better than that, my little slut," she teased her. "Ask me like you really mean it!"

Emma wriggled and moaned; now half mad with passion. "Pleeease Miss Duncan. Please make me cum. I'll do anything!"

Amy smiled. "I know you will cupcake. We'll come to that a little later." She lowered her head and sucked hard on the girl's clitty, as her fingers began to flash in and out of her juicy slit.

"Oh! Oh! Ohhhhhh!" Emma's orgasm simply erupted. Her body spasmed, her head shook violently from side to side and her pussy clamped hard around her teacher's fingers.

It took several minutes before Emma could open her eyes but when she did, she found herself looking straight into the deep blue eyes of a stranger. A man! She was still too half soaked to panic but she realised he could see her at her most vulnerable. Her thighs were still open and she could feel the juices drying on her inner thighs. Her hands were up by her head in a completely submissive pose; like a baby sleeping. She saw he was a big rugged and very handsome man and his eyes were fixed on her erect nipples as he licked his lips.

"This is my lover, Jared," Amy said softly. "He's been watching us for the last half hour and now he wants you. Is that all right?"

Emma said nothing, she was still in shock and Jared took her silence as consent. Leaning over, his lips found her own and he kissed her more warmly and passionately than the youngster could have imagined. His hands came up and gripped her young breasts tightly, making the young woman quiver.

Eventually Jared came up for air. Without saying a word, he took the girl's hand to pull her up off the bed and then guided her down on to her knees. Face to face with his bulging crotch, Emma didn't need to be told what to do. Slowly unzipping him, she put her hand in his fly and wrapped her hand around a thick rod of meat. Drawing it out, her jaw dropped when she saw what she was holding. Jared was built!

"Put it in your mouth and get it nice and hard," Amy told her and Emma did exactly as she was told, even though she couldn't imagine it being any harder. The helmet was as big as her little mouth and it was all she could do to take the first two inches, leaving at least eight outside. She began to slowly rub her hand up and down the shaft, instinctively wanking the older man.

Amy stood back and watched her cute little student struggling to get her man into her mouth. It was entertaining to watch but time to move things on a little. Kneeling down beside her, she took hold of Jared's cock by the root and pushed Emma away. "Watch and learn my little kitten," she said, immediately swallowing the long fat cock in one. The teenager's eyes almost popped out her head at this expert demonstration of sword swallowing. Amy bobbed her head several times to thoroughly massage her fiancé's cock and then handed him back to her protégée. "Try a little harder," she said meaningfully.

This time Emma took another couple of inches and her eyes watered as the man meat bumped against the back of her throat. She instinctively backed off, only to feel Amy's hand on the back of her head. "I said try harder!" she said fiercely, pushing her back on to the shaft. Emma gagged and spluttered as the cockhead wedged itself in her gullet. And then it was through. She couldn't breathe and had to concentrate on not panicking but she was holding that enormous cock in her throat. Amy held the girl's chin and extended her neck a little to open her throat more. "Better, my dear. Well done," she said, stroking Emma's throat to ease the passage.

Eventually Jared's cock was completely embedded in Emma's throat and he quickly backed off to let her breathe when he sensed she was about to completely run out of air. She gulped down some cool, fresh air and it was the best feeling in the world as the middle-aged man pushed himself into her again. As he picked up his pace, Amy knelt behind her student to squeeze her tits and guide her head; encouraging her to bob back and forth faster and faster.

"Fuck!" Jared spoke for the first time. "Her mouth is so fucking hot, I'm gonna blow a nut in her throat if I don't stop now."

"If you think her mouth's hot," said Amy. "Wait 'til you try her cunt. Fancy popping a virgin?" she added coyly.

"You think?" Jared picked Emma up and threw her on to her back on the bed, before climbing on top of her. She felt that hard and rubbery cock head search for her opening, before it lodged itself firmly in her slit and the pressure started to build.

As Jared entered her, Emma felt her pussy mouth stretch and it was really bloody painful. "Uhhhhh!" She thrashed her head and moaned as he got further and further inside her love tunnel, widening her all the way up. There was nothing pleasurable about this at all and the teenager decided there and then that this would be the first and last time she would have sex with a man. And then he stopped and she felt him wedged against her, realising he had come up against her maidenhead. Jared grabbed her head in both hands and made damned sure she was looking into his eyes as he flexed his hips and obliterated her hymen. "Arrrrgh!" That moment was one of the most painful experiences of her young life. It was horrible.

Jared was moving slowly inside her and Emma suddenly realised it wasn't horrible anymore. Her pussy was tingling and really felt very good. She could feel every bump and ridge on this man's massive tool as he continued to ream her little twat out and the pressure was still intense; but it just felt good! She heard a really horny little guttural moaning: "Uh! Uh! Uh!" And then she realised the noise was her! She was the horny little slut who was rapidly getting delirious on the big cock of a man easily old enough to be her father and who was the boyfriend of her English teacher; the woman now suckling on her sensitive nipples.

With the best will in the world, Jared was not going to last long. He was balls deep in the cutest little girl he had ever known and his woman was now sucking her improbably large tits. Emma was so tight her meat was turning itself inside out with his cock, as it squeezed the juice out of him. He was going to blow soon and hard. The only question was where he was going to put it.

Amy answered the question for him. Bending over Emma's face, she sucked on the girl's lip for a moment and then fixed her with a stare. "Jared's going to spunk inside you now Sweety," she said. "Let's see if we can knock you up and make this cute little belly swell." She stroked the young woman just above where her fiancé was pounding into her.

Emma was horrified. That was possibly the worst thing she had heard but somehow it was also incredibly horny. The idea of of being so under the control of this woman, and now her man as well, that *she* would decide when she would get pregnant was intoxifying! The more she thought about it, the hotter she got and then…, "Oh! Oh! Oh my God! Yeeeees!" She came so hard it actually knocked her out for a couple of seconds. Her body spasmed and her pussy locked hard around the fat cock inside her.

That was enough for Jared. He reached up to grab Emma's fat tits; knocking his girlfriend out the way. One more hard thrust and then his cock was discharging cum like a fire hose; straight into the virgin's womb.

Their twin orgasms seem to last an eternity. Eventually Jared collapsed on top of her and Emma felt her own body start to relax a little. The huge amount of cum inside her pussy was already starting to leak out and when the big man knelt up and pulled himself out, the dribble became a river.

"Mmmm! That's mine!" Amy purred, crawling back between her young lover's legs and lapping at the juices.

Emma was now a woman and as she lay back and enjoyed the feeling of her teacher licking the cum out of her slit, she wondered what she had to do to get detention all week..

TEACHER LEARNS A LESSON
Teacher Sex # 2

Craig made sure to slam the door loudly on his way in. He knew he was expected but didn't want to surprise his lover. Sarah had been playing with her latest submissive, single mother Stacie for the past few hours and she should now be ready for him.

They certainly had an interesting relationship, businessman Craig and his teacher fiancée, Sarah. Both had sex drives that went through the roof and they were both dominant. Sarah naturally took the submissive role between them but she needed to seek out true submissives from time to time to get it out of her system. Naturally Craig was only too happy to play with her toys too; at least the women. He had no interest in other men.

And the woman Sarah had waiting for him in their big playroom in the cellar was a prize. Twenty three year old Stacie was about five foot two high, blonde hair and pretty face, with a lovely curvy body. A body that was completely naked and available. Sarah had explored every last inch of the gorgeous creature. She had spanked and subdued her, licked out and ridden her. She was now completely passive and would do whatever her Mistress commanded her to.

He didn't go straight downstairs though. There was plenty of time for that. Grabbing a cold bottle of beer from the fridge, Craig sat in front of the huge television screen in the lounge and flicked through the channels to their own CCTV circuit. Sitting back and sucking on the cold bottle, he watched his lover playing with her new toy. Sarah was lying back on the bed and Stacie, completely free of her bonds was now on her hands and knees, licking the older woman out. His fiancée was following her usual cycle and close to having her dominance urges satisfied for a while. Time for him to step in. Picking up his beer, he made his way downstairs.

As he stepped through the cellar door, Craig was confronted by a cracking sight. Stacie hadn't moved from her position on camera and her naked arse was pointing straight up towards him. Her legs were slightly parted and he could see the moist pink flesh between them. It was an offer he couldn't refuse. Climbing onto the bed behind her, he rested a big cool hand on her hot buttock and unzipped himself. "She's very pretty darling," he said to Sarah. "Is she as tight as she looks?"

"Find out for yourself," said Sarah as she held tightly to a struggling Stacie. "Hold still you silly tart while your Master takes you," she said sharply to the younger woman.

Craig pushed himself slowly into Stacie's fragrant pussy. She was indeed tight; he could feel every fold of flesh as it bumped over his penis. Stacie started to make interesting little noises that were muffled by Sarah's twat. It was hard to discern what, if anything, she was saying but it didn't sound like dissent. As he gripped the young mother tightly by the hips and rocked into her, Sarah extricated herself, clearly sated and moved to the side to watch her new pet being fucked.

"Ooooh!" Stacie's face being freed from Sarah's twat, she started to make a lot of noise. It had been quite a while since she had had a cock inside her and Craig's was well above average size. He held her tightly and began to hump her hard, their bodies coming together with a very erotic *slap, slap,* sound.

"Fuck, you are tight," he exclaimed as he reamed her pussy out. She was so small, her pussy held tightly to his cock and seemed to turn inside out each time he withdrew, to be pushed back into place so hard she wheezed with each penetration. He knew he wasn't going to last long on this first fuck but that was fine, he could get back up very quickly and intended playing with this toy all night.

Instinctively realising he was going to come, Stacie turned her head and spoke to her new Master for the first time. "Please don't come in me," she begged. "I'm not on the pill."

Before Craig could say anything, Sarah had grasped Stacie's face in one hand and pushed her head back on the bed. "Your Master will come wherever he wants and you'll enjoy it like a good slut," she said.

"Yes Miss," said Stacie from the mattress, her voice trembling as she began to cum.

Craig slapped her arse, held her hips tightly and thrust himself hard into her pussy as his balls tightened and he filled the submissive woman with his spunk. That tipped Stacie completely over the edge and she trembled all over as she shouted out her climax. "Oh, yes!"

Craig withdrew and called Sarah over to take his softening cock in her mouth to thoroughly clean it, before moving on to Stacie's pussy, which was dripping with their mutual juices. As his woman licked and sucked, he got off the bed and pushed his cock back into his pants.

Looking through the extensive racks of whips, floggers, dildos and restraints, Craig found what he wanted and threw them all in a pile on the bed. "It's been a while since I've had two sex toys to play with," he said as he grabbed Sarah and buckled a set of sturdy leather cuffs to her wrists at the front of her body. "She may be your Mistress," he said to Stacie, "but she's my slave. Watch while I remind her of that fact." He walked her out to the centre of the room where a handy rope hung from the ceiling and clipped her cuffs into it. Pulling on the other end through a ratchet, he then strung her body up tautly until she was on her toes.

Sarah was less than impressed with the turn of events but knew better than to struggle or protest. She just fixed her face with a stubborn grimace and accepted that her Dom session had just turned into a sub one. The look of defiance didn't escape Craig's eagle eye though. "It looks to me like someone needs reminding of their role around here," he said sternly as he cruelly twisted her rubbery nipples between his fingers.

"Nggug," Sarah tried hard to bite her lip but the sudden rush of pain to her nips was too much. She swung helplessly from side to side on her tip toes as her lover pulled and squeezed. Abruptly he released them and the sudden rush of blood caused her to release another little cry. "Oooh!"

Craig picked up a riding crop and ran it up and down his fiancées body a few times, flicking at her stiff nipples with the loop at the end and then rubbing it between her inflamed pussy lips until she began to squirm. "Pay attention, Stacie," he said to the younger woman. "The tautness of Sarah's body will accentuate the kiss of the whip. She remembers that well and that's why she is having to concentrate hard to be obedient and wait for the first lash. See how her body trembles." Sarah's body was trembling alright. Stacie crawled to the end of the bed and cupped her chin in her hands as she watched the ice cool Mistress who had manipulated her with such ease reduced in a few minutes to complete subservience by the man whose seed was dribbling down her leg. The power of the man enthralled her.

Without warning the crop struck Sarah across both of her rock hard nipples. She jerked with surprise at the sudden sensation and despite herself she couldn't hold back a cry of pain and pleasure, "Aaargh!" She swayed desperately from left to right on her toes.

Craig turned to Stacie. "Come here child," he said softly but firmly. She jumped off the bed and walked over. "Put your finger in her pussy and tell me what you feel."

Stacie parted Sarah's petals with her middle finger and her finger glided inside. "She's very, very wet," she said with a little surprise in her voice.

"She's very, very horny," replied Craig. "You didn't realise but Sarah is very submissive. She only found her dominant side with mousey women like you when she had been my pet for several years. You'd like to fuck her wouldn't you?"

Stacie dropped her head and said nothing. She'd already experienced almost every carnal act with Sarah that she could imagine but she knew exactly what he meant; would she like to be on top with Sarah? Before she could think of an appropriate reply, Craig was speaking again. "Go and fetch the stuff off the bed," he said as he lowered Sarah so she could stand flat on her feet with some slack in the rope.

Stacie collected up the collection of bondage gear and handed it over. Craig quickly secured her wrists with the same sort of leather cuffs that Sarah had on and then picked up a couple of curious, long, thin metal tubes. As Stacie watched carefully, he pulled on each of Sarah's long nipples in turn and slipped the cylinders over them, holding and releasing a small button to capture her teats in their metal teeth. She yelped like a puppy as the first one went on and just grimaced with the second. Stacie's eyes widened as it became apparent to her what was going into the identical other ends of the long tubes.

Craig slackened Sarah's rope right off and then grabbed Stacie by her cuffs. "Come on then puppy," he said, attaching the ring on the cuffs to the same clip holding Sarah in place. Hauling on the rope, he stopped when Stacie was stretched out as far as she could without getting up on to her toes. Sarah still had a bit of slack in her arms to move around but Stacie was now the one as taut as a bowstring. The rope brought the girls abruptly together but their difference in height meant Stacie was almost mouth to tit with Sarah.

Reaching between the young women, Craig found Stacie's tits and began to roughly pull and stretch the nipples. She moaned and writhed around in her bondage but couldn't bring herself to complain. Once he was satisfied they were long and hard enough, he pulled on the left nipple, found the end of the tube, which just reached down far enough, and snapped it into place on the tender flesh.

"Arrrgh!" Stacie was ready for it but she had no idea how much it was going to hurt. She gritted her teeth and waited for the other one to connect but she didn't have to wait for long. "Oh, shit!" she exclaimed.

Craig stepped back and realised he needed to make Stacie a little taller for what he had in mind. Retrieving an aerobic step from the back of the room, he put it on the floor and encouraged Stacie to step up on it. That relieved a bit of the pressure on the girls' tits and he heard a sigh of relief as she got up. More importantly, it raised her high enough for him to fuck her arse without having to contort himself into an uncomfortable position. He had a couple of other adjustments to make first though.

Grabbing some lube, he greased up a long, jelly-like double-headed dildo. Holding it up to Stacie's eyes-line he asked, "do you want to guess where this is going to go?" Dropping to his knees, he reached between the shorter woman's legs and began to feed it into his girlfriend's pussy, holding her firmly in place with a hand on her arse. Once it was in as far as he could get it, he introduced the other end to Stacie's twat. He felt the difference in tightness straight away and despite herself, she began to buck and whimper. Rather than punishing her at this stage, Craig rubbed gently on her clit to relax her and gently but firmly continued to push it in.

Before long the big jelly cock was wedged well and truly inside the two cunts, with just an inch or so showing. Stacie was still an inch or so shorter than Sarah which meant a flex of her hips was enough to drive the phallus into Sarah. Stepping behind the young woman, he slapped her hard on the arse and chuckled as the effect of the dildo moving meant Sarah moaned more loudly than Stacie.

Craig had one final touch before he started the fun and games. Reaching into a storage box, he pulled out a contraption he had got custom-made and hadn't had chance to try out yet. It was a double-sided penis gag. Feeding the long and fat cock-shaped rubber into both girls' mouths, he attached the harnesses around their heads and pulled them tight. As an afterthought, he grabbed the lube again and massaged plenty into both women's back-passages. Stacie really wriggled for that one and Craig noticed just how tight she was.

Stepping back, he looked at his work. The girls were now attached at the mouth, tit and pussy and Stacie was in an ideal position to start fucking Sarah, she just needed a little encouragement. Running a hand down each of their backs and over the curve of their buttocks, he sighed. "Fuck girls, I'm really going to enjoy you both now." He went back to his rack of floggers and whips and took his time in selecting the right one, holding up the multi-tailed soft suede cat so that both women could see it.

Stepping behind Stacie again, he briefly cupped her pussy in his hand to feel her anticipation and then, with a well-aimed backhand flick, brought the tails down across both buttocks. The blow set of a chain reaction: a muffled cry from Stacie, a violent jerking of her hips and then a muffled moan from Sarah. Craig was proud of himself; the system worked perfectly. Stepping further back, he began a rhythmic striping of her arse, which translated into the start of a good fucking for both of his girls but especially Sarah.

After a dozen easy blows, Craig paused and saw that Stacie's hips were moving of their own accord. He put the whip down and rested his hand gently on her hot bottom. "That's it little one," he breathed into her ear. "Give the little tramp a good fucking for me." Removing his clothes as he watched, he gave his hard cock a few rubs and then moved behind Sarah. Positioning himself carefully, he grabbed her hips and shoved himself violently into her arse, completing her double-penetration.

For several minutes, Craig relished the hot, buttery feeling of his girlfriend's back passage. He was perfectly in time with Stacie's now accomplished humping, which was just poetry in motion, her hips rotating, pulling on their tits and stuffing the dildo down both girls' throats with each revolution. He was just contemplating changing over to Stacie's virgin bottom when Sarah began to shudder and moan into her gag. He upped his pace and managed a couple more strokes before she came hard. Her bottom clamped tightly around his cock and her legs literally gave way, leaving her suspended by her arms, tits, cunt and arse. Craig withdrew, his cock still hard. He was going to finish in Stacie's virgin hole but he'd decided to have her out of bondage to increase the fun.

Removing the head harnesses and nipple tubes, Craig lowered the rope and unclipped them from it, leaving the girls to work the tight dildo out of their sore twats. Removing Sarah's cuffs only, he barked an order at her. "Take her into the bathroom and give her an enema."

Sarah snapped straight back into Mistress mode. Grabbing Stacie's wrists, she pulled her behind her into the small bathroom, bent her over the shower cubicle and clipped her cuffs onto a bar near the floor. Picking up a pre-prepared enema bag, she hooked it on to the shower rail and worked the nozzle into her puckered arsehole. "That's it sweety, just relax," she said soothingly as the nozzle popped through the girl's sphincter. "Yow!" Stacie yelped as her muscle gave in. "That just feels… so weird," she added as the fluid started to fill her bowel.

"That's right sweetheart," said Sarah, rubbing the younger woman's lower stomach in circular motions to help the motion. "You'll get used to it; it's really not so bad. You just need to relax."

"It's not bad at all" replied Stacie dreamily.

The bag emptied in no time at all and by this time Stacie already felt she had an urgent need to release it. "I'll come back for you in ten minutes," said Sarah as she slapped the younger woman on the arse. She knew she was being pretty cruel, having experienced the feeling herself many times before. She closed the door behind her and went to see how she could best serve her Master while she was waiting.

Craig was watching some porn on the TV. "Ah, there you are," he said as Sarah re-entered the room. "I could do with a massage while I'm waiting." He turned over on to his belly and stretched while Sarah rubbed oil into her hands. "Umm, that's good," he sighed as her practiced hands moved in big circles over the skin on his back. She worked his muscles hard until he turned over and then she started on his chest and shoulders. "That's good too," he smirked, "but maybe you should go a little lower?" Sarah glanced down to where his cock was rising again. His intent was clear; she moved down his body and took it completely in her mouth, tasting the residue of her own bottom.

Having been distracted, Sarah left her pet somewhat longer than the intended ten minutes. By the time she re-entered the bathroom, Stacie was hopping from one leg to the next, desperate to avoid an accident. "Pleeease," she pleaded.

"Don't worry, little one," Sarah chuckled. "It's time." She unshackled the young woman from the shower and sat her down on the loo. Stacie looked at her for a desperate moment, hoping she could be left in privacy and then nature took its course; her bottom exploded into the toilet.

When Sarah was content Stacie had finished, she wiped her down and then gave her a quick rinse in the shower. Rubbing her down with the towel, she took her face in her hand and looked her in the eyes. "Listen to me sweetheart. Your first anal sex can be the most wonderful experience in the world or the most horrible. I'm going to help you make it wonderful but you need to do your best to relax, do you understand?" Stacie nodded.

Sarah unfastened Stacie's cuffs and fetched a couple of items from the bathroom cabinet. First of all she greased the girl's arsehole again and then she held a vial under her nose. "Breathe deeply, petal," she said in a soothing voice. "This will help your sphincter relax."

Stacie breathed in and felt her head spin. As she recovered, she realised her lover was on her knees, lapping at her pussy again. Sarah ate her out until she started leaking lots of juice into her mouth and then judged her ready. Standing up she slapped her arse. "Go and get your buggering sweetheart," she said, propelling her back into the bedroom.

.

A SPANKING FOR TEACHER
Teacher Sex #3

It was the usual sort of bedlam in Key Stage One English and it took a few minutes for Sarah to get the class settled behind their books. Once they were reading, she sat back and thought about her weekend spent enjoying her yummy mummy, Stacie, along with her masterful boyfriend. She had drifted into a world of her own when she realised with a start there was a little girl standing next to her chair.

"Sir said to give you this Miss," she mumbled before disappearing back through the classroom door.

The note was from the headmaster; curt and to the point: *I wish to speak to you about an incident during parents evening. Please be in my office at 5pm sharp!*

Shit! How could he possibly know about Stacie? Sarah's mind was wandering and she looked up to see several inquisitive six year old faces staring back at her.

Her mind continued to wander throughout the whole day and by the time five o'clock had come around, she decided the authoritative head teacher was referring about something else entirely. There was no way he could possibly have known about Stacie. There was probably a fight in the corridor or something! She finished tidying her classroom, smoothed her dress down over her supple body and marched off to Mr Pritchard's office with her head held high.

"Have a seat Miss Hadrian." Mrs Harris, the prim and proper secretary pointed to the two child-sized chairs outside the head's door. She struggled on to one and held tightly to her skirt but it rode up her thighs nonetheless. She glanced at the clock and saw she still had five minutes to go. That was a relief. Mr Pritchard hated tardiness.

Ten minutes later and she was still waiting, Sarah could hear the buzz of voices through the door and guessed there were about half a dozen adults in there. Presumably he was running over on another meeting. As she sat waiting, Sarah began to regret wearing the bright blue, stretchy jersey dress she had decided upon that morning. It was just a little short to meet the strict headmaster's high standards but then she hadn't expected to be summoned to his office that day. As she sat waiting to be called in, on a chair that was several inches too low, she could feel the hem working its way up her thigh. She crossed her legs and that immediately made matters a lot worse. All that fidgeting around made her aware that her bladder was pretty full and she also regretted not remembering to have a wee. Considering whether she could quickly nip away, she glanced at the clock and saw it was already twelve minutes past. Knowing her luck, she would be called in as soon as she left and then there would be hell to pay. She would have to wait until after the appointment but of course, now she was thinking about it, she suddenly felt desperate for the toilet and began rubbing her thighs together to ease the pressure. She fidgeted around on the hard little seat again and her skirt rode up to the top of her thigh.

All of a sudden the door opened with a crash. Clive Reynolds, the PE teacher stood in the doorway. "The headmaster is ready for you now Sarah," he boomed. Sarah jumped up and yanked her dress back down to below her knees. She walked into the office to see the headmaster seated at his huge oak desk, flanked by four other members of staff.

"Stand there Sarah," the headmaster indicated a square of carpet in front of her desk and she sensed Mr Reynolds moving up behind her. "I'll come straight to the point," Mr Pritchard continued. "I know you were engaged in inappropriate behaviour with one of our parents after the parents evening."

Sarah's jaw nearly hit the floor. How could he possibly know that unless Stacie told him! She opened her mouth to speak and then closed it again at a withering look from the Head. He continued talking. "We know Miss Hadrian that you seduced Miss Smith, a vulnerable single mother, in your classroom and having corrupted her, engaged in a number of unnatural practices on school property. Do you deny it?"

Sarah was speechless and merely shrugged so the Head went on. "I have enough evidence to sack you on the spot and ensure you will never work as a teacher again but I'm a firm believer in the short, sharp shock and so I'm prepared to take another approach if you are willing?"

Sarah had no idea what he was talking about and said so. "I'm sorry Sir, I don't follow."

"You are pretty dim for a teacher sometimes Sarah. I am proposing corporal punishment in this instance and for that I need your consent. The alternative is you leave the building now; never to return! Do I have your consent?"

"… Are you saying you want to spank me?" Sarah had been spanked many times by her fiancé and Master but that was always in the privacy of their own home and normally alone. Even for a switch like her, the idea of being spanked by her boss in public was a step too far.

"I am saying I will spank you just for starters. By the time you leave my office, I guarantee you will have learned your lesson young lady. Now, do I have your consent?"

"I don't see you've left me any alternative."

"Good girl," replied the Headmaster, pushing a pen and paper across the desk. "Sign this!"

Sarah quickly scanned the form and saw it was her consent to receiving corporal punishment. She quickly scrawled her signature at the bottom and pushed it back across the huge desk.

The Head picked the paper up without checking it and dropped it into his top drawer. "Good!" he said. "Let's get on with it. Bend over, facing towards me and grip your ankles."

Sarah gulped and did exactly as ordered. As her hands reached down her legs, she could feel her dress riding up higher and higher, until she was sure her knickers must be on display. More significantly though, the act of leaning forward was putting more pressure on her bladder and it was all Sarah could do to not pee on the carpet. The Headmaster spoke again. "Mademoiselle Labarte, perhaps you would like to take the honours and start the proceedings?" Sarah was surprised and a little relieved. She thought her spanking was going to be at the strong hand of Mr Reynolds.

The young French mistress could hardly contain her glee. Walking around the desk, she patted Sarah's raised rump a little possessively, before slowly pulling the hem of her dress up the rest of the way, to reveal her little white panties. "Knickers up or down Monsieur?" Celine asked in her cultured accent.

"Leave them up for now my dear," replied the Head. "There's plenty of time later," he added ominously.

Celine was clearly an old hand at spanking. Resting one small hand on the small of Sarah's back, she pushed down a little to splay the older woman's bottom out even further. "It would please me a great deal if you call them out in French for me, Sarah," she purred as she caressed the cotton-covered flesh. The others thought that idea hilarious.

Smack! The slight Mademoiselle Labarte packed a blow far out of proportion to her size. "Arrrgh!" Sarah yelled out loud.

"Tut! Tut!" Celine admonished her. "I didn't hear a 'un'. I shall have to double the amount!"

This time, as she hand came down across Sarah's left buttock there was no hesitation. "Un!" she cried.

The blows came thick and fast. "Deux, trois, quatre." They hurt like hell but all Sarah could think about were the tops of her thighs pressing against her bladder. The need was more than urgent now and she thought she felt a little drip fall on to her gusset. She was petrified that Celine might notice.

After what seemed a lifetime, the spanking finished. Without being told to, Sarah quickly stood up to relieve the pressure and her dress fell back into place. The look of the Headmaster's face told her he was unimpressed with her initiative in this case. "Now that Mademoiselle Labarte has warmed you up," he announced. "It's time for your punishment to start. Step forward and bend over the desk." Sarah did as she was bid and bent so far forward, she felt the wood against her thighs and then the table top was pressing against her bladder, creating a pressure even worse than before. She couldn't hold on much longer.

Out of the corner of her eye, Sarah saw Mr Reynolds select a heavy cane from the Headmaster's cabinet and then swish it through the air for effect, so close to her face that she felt the air move. All of a sudden, Sarah realised she was going to get a caning and the idea was too much for her. Her legs buckled underneath her and her bladder relaxed. Before she could stop it, a torrent of piss drenched her panties and ran down her leg.

"Oh la la!" The shock in the French teacher's voice was apparent to everyone and although she was one of only three people in the room who knew what had happened at that moment, it didn't take long for the others to figure it out.

Sarah looked up and caught the Headmaster's eye and it was if he had read her mind in that instance. "Have you wet yourself, you dirty little girl?" he asked in a cold tone.

"I-I'm sorry Sir, I couldn't help myself..." Sarah stuttered, before being interrupted by the Head.

"Stand up and take off your soiled knickers, you filthy little slut," he snarled.

By this time, Sarah's face was burning crimson. She stood up and peeled the damp panties down her legs and off, over her heels. The Headmaster pointed to a spot on his desk and she dropped them there. "Bend back over the desk and reach across as far as you can." Sarah pressed her thighs to the side of the desk and her big breasts to the top, as she stretched as far as she could, suddenly anxious to please. Mr Pritchard picked up her underwear with a disdainful expression on his face. "We may as well put these to good use," he said. "Open your mouth."

Was there to be no end to her humiliation? Sarah opened her mouth wide and as expected the Head crumpled her damp panties into a ball and shoved them so far into her mouth, she began to gag. The pee seeped out of the material and dripped down her throat – an acidic bitter taste that was just simply unpleasant!

"I think we are ready to begin the punishment, Mr Reynolds," said the Head, grabbing Sarah's wrists and holding her firmly in place. Moments later, a *swish* and Sarah felt a white hot pain, right across the crease at the bottom of her arse. She couldn't contain herself and spat the knickers out. "Arrrgh! Oh my God, no!"

"That was one," said the Headmaster smugly. "Your punishment was twelve but it's just doubled as you didn't keep your gag in. But perhaps we can find something a little more effective?" He stood up and unzipped his fly to produce the biggest cock Sarah had seen in her life. It must have been a foot long and was definitely too wide for her to wrap her hand around. *She had no idea!* Gripping it in one hand, he pushed it towards her face as he held her head in place with the other.

Sarah struggled to get her mouth around the Headmaster's cock but it was no use. As he forced her face down into his groin, she began to whimper like a puppy. The Head looked at his PE teacher. "I think she needs some encouragement," he chuckled as he grabbed the young woman's nose and lifted. Another swishing sound, her arse lit up again and as Sarah's mouth and throat opened for another cry, Mr Pritchard stuffed his meat in.

Sarah was now stretched over the desk, with her bare arse pointed towards the room and already bright red. Her hands rested on the Headmaster's muscular upper thighs and she was literally impaled on his cock by the throat. The steady blows now began to rain down on her arse.

"This is quite a performance," said Celine at the sixth blow of the cane. "She wriggles so nicely. It is very horny."

"I suppose you want to fuck her," said the Headmaster nonchalantly as he thrust into the hapless teacher's throat. "Why don't you see if she's wet and open yet?"

Completely preoccupied with trying to breath around the monstrous meat shaft in her airway, Sarah had almost managed to block out the intense pain in her rump but her attention was completely seized by the French mistress's long fingers as they slid straight up inside her and twisted around a few times.

"Alors! She is soaked. I think that Miss Hadrian wants some cock!"

"Well, she is due another fourteen blows of the cane first," mused the Headmaster. "But I suppose we could suspend the punishment in the interests of staff morale. "I think it's only fair that Mr Reynolds goes first, as he's fluffed her up!"

Seconds later, Sarah felt strong hands on her hips and pressure against her pussy. Slowly but surely the PE teacher's cock opened up her petals and pressed inside. His wasn't the biggest cock she had taken but it was very knobbly and seemed to have a bend in it. As it crept up her love tunnel, it scraped along her g spot and she jumped as though electrocuted.

Pushing up on to her hands, the horny teacher found herself being pushed to and fro by the cocks taking her from either end.

The massive shaft in her throat moved a little more freely once her muscles had relaxed a little and the one in her cunt sent magical tingles through her clitoris. As she rocked between the men, Sarah fully appreciated the expression *spit roast* as she had a mental image of being suspended over a fire like a suckling pig.

The men came almost together. As Sarah drank down her headmaster's thick, salty sperm, the crooked cock coughed and spat a large wad straight into her womb. As she expected, the PE teacher was quickly replaced but not by who she expected. "I 'ave been looking forward to this all day," purred Celine as she eased a thick rubber cock into Sarah's twat. Her delicate hands rested on the teacher's firm buttocks as the big strap on began to ream out her pussy.

"Oh! Oh! Oh!" As Celine rammed her fake cock into Sarah, each thrust pushed a guttural moan out from deep in the young woman's throat. The younger woman's long finger's found her slut's clitoris and she played it like a violin. Sarah arched her back and shivered with passion. "Oh my God, yes!"

Suddenly, Celine withdrew and with a strength the belied her size, span Sarah around and whipped her dress off over her head. Unsnapping her bra, she dipped her head to suck on the primary teacher's big tits, while continuing to finger her. Edging her back to the desk, she coaxed her on to her back, spread her legs and climbed up on to the desk herself. Crouching on the edge of the platform, she fed the rubber dong back into the waiting cunt to fuck the horny teacher with little rabbit strokes.

Sarah lasted no more than another two minutes. As the younger woman pulled on her nipples and humped her with short, fast strokes, she came explosively. A red mist fell before her eyes, her whole body began to shake and she simply screamed. "Arrrrrgh!!"

Once Celine had finished with her, Sarah was fucked hard by both the year four and year six teachers, before the Headmaster was confident her pussy could take his monstrous cock. He rested her legs on his shoulders and slowly but surely forced his way into her. Sarah's breath came in short pants as her birth canal opened up to an unprecedented size. As he finally bottomed out, Mr Pritchard leaned forward and whispered in her ear. "Craig sends his love and wishes you a happy birthday."

Sarah's eyes snapped open. "You know my fiancé?"

The Headmaster chuckled as he began to force himself in and out of the deliciously tight pussy. "Craig and I were army mates together; we've known each other for years. He's given me a cracking film of what he did to you and Stacie. Would you like to see it?"

"So, that's how you found out about her," Sarah grunted underneath him. She got no reply as Mr Pritchard focused on pleasuring the woman of his best friend. His abdominal muscles rippled with each powerful thrust of his hips; driving her along the rough table top. A crescendo of noise began to build; a slapping of flesh the Headmaster slammed into his favourite teacher, her moaning filling the room as she climbed towards her peak of pleasure.

With a triumphant cry, the Headmaster filled Sarah's love tunnel with what seemed to be pints of hot spunk. This pushed her into her orgasm and she began to tremble and shake like an epileptic. He collapsed on top of her heaving breasts of found her lips with his own. When he finally found his breath, he whispered to her again. "I'd better let you get home then. I'll be coming to visit tonight so we can have you together!"

PET TEACHER
Sub Teacher # 2

I looked at the clock again. The hour hand seemed to be moving like the second hand normally did. I tried to focus on the class of eager teens in front of me but all I could think of was what Mr and Mrs Arnold were going to do to me once that hand hit the four and the weekend began.

Mr and Mrs Arnold. *Master and Mistress!* That's what they were now. Not just the parents of one of my students. They owned me like a slave, or a pet. And it was all because I did some glamour work to pay my student bills five years ago. Somehow the perverted couple had found a video online that looked like I was involved in porn. Regardless of the truth, I knew the head teacher and board of governors would regard it as incompatible with my employment as a teacher. I couldn't afford to lose my career and so I found myself helpless in their hands.

The clock hands found three thirty in no time at all. I dismissed my class and organised the classroom ready for Monday morning.

My phone was on my desk and I couldn't take my eyes off it. Finally it rang.

"Hello slut!" It was Mrs Arnold.

"Hello Mistress," I said as respectfully as I could. I couldn't afford to take the risk of upsetting her again.

"I'm outside. Be there in five minutes."

"Yes Mistress." The idea of disobeying wasn't even an option for me. This masterful couple now owned me. It had started with the material in their hands but became something entirely different. Their power over me was like a drug. The sex was much, much more than just sex. The orgasms they created in me nearly knocked me unconscious and they came hard and regularly. I had arranged for my teenage son to stay over with a friend. I was theirs for the whole weekend.

The black Mercedes with its tinted windows was at the school gate, as though I was their child they were picking up. And in a way I suppose I was! Once with them, I am completely dependent on the couple. I walked up to the driver's side, hoping no one was watching.

The window scrolled down silently. "Get in the back and kneel up on the seat," my Mistress told me and pressed the button to close it again. I got in as instructed and reached for the seatbelt. "You won't need that," she snapped and pulled the big car away from the curb.

I knelt up, pulling my shoulders back and pushing my bust out in the way I know my Mistress expected. She said nothing for a few minutes but I was very aware of her watching me in the rear view mirror. Finally she spoke again. "Unbutton your blouse," she said; "slowly!" I obeyed, of course. Slowly working the small buttons open, I kept my chest thrust out as far as possible and made my movements as sexy as possible. I knew that was what she wanted.

The buttons unfastened, I pulled the ends out of my skirt and opened it as far as possible to reveal my swelling, silky bra. "All the way off," I was ordered. "The bra too!" I unbuttoned my cuffs and slipped the expensive blouse off to place it on the seat behind me. I couldn't see Mistress's expression but I knew she liked my breasts, so I didn't hang around. I reached behind me, unhooked the clasp and let the cups fall off my tits.

"Hands under your arse and push your tits out!" I followed her instructions to the letter, although I felt very self-conscious as we slowly drove through traffic. There were people walking past only a few feet from my naked womanhood and even though I knew they couldn't see a thing through the dark glass, it was of course completely transparent to me and subconsciously, it seemed as though all these business men, housewives and groups of youths could see me just as well.

Louise said nothing for another ten minutes. She just glanced at me when she could and enjoyed seeing my exposed tit flesh. I could see my reflection in the dark screen of a seatback TV and knew exactly what a picture I made. My long nipples were rock hard and stuck out obscenely from the small pink areolae. My big tits were very firm and stuck proudly from my chest. There was no sign of sag there; I looked after myself.

The car slowed again and I looked out to see we were in a very rough part of town. A black suburb! The vehicle approached a large group of youths, smoking on a street corner and as we stopped at the lights right next to them, I once again imagined what would happen if they could see me. They were mostly looking at the car, which looked out of place in this poor area. A tall, muscular black boy seemed to be looking straight at me when, suddenly, the window began to silently move downwards.

Oh fuck! I desperately wanted to cover myself but didn't dare move my hands from under my buttocks. The first boy yelled and caught the attention of the others, who went ballistic. The insults began to fly.

"You can touch if you like, boys and girls!" Mistress had her window down too. "Don't try and get in the car and don't damage my property!"

They didn't have to be told twice. My upper body was suddenly covered with dark hands; all squeezing, pinching and stroking. I felt utterly, utterly horny!

"That's all folks," Louise called. The window came up and the car pulled away. I was now very flustered and a little sweaty. She glanced in the mirror and laughed. "You look like you've been gangbanged already," she said ominously. "Put your blouse back on but leave your bra off… Your panties can go too," she added as an afterthought. I quickly pulled my thin cotton top on; very aware that my dark pink nipples would be completely visible through the white material. I slipped my knickers off, to leave them with the matching bra on the seat and got back into the kneeling position. "Here," my Mistress called over her shoulder and handed back a blindfold. "Put that on and make sure you can't see through it." I did as she told me and then waited patiently for whatever was coming next.

I lost track of time as I knelt there in darkness and listened to the noises of the car. I heard us turn on to a motorway or fast dual carriageway and then leaving it after one or two exits. The traffic noise gradually fell behind us and eventually we turned on to a crunchy gravel drive before coming to a stop.

The car door opened and I felt hands on my neck and shoulders. Something was wrapped tightly around my neck and I was pulled out of the car by it; a collar I realised. My hands were fastened behind me and then I was led away from the car by some unidentified person.

"What have you got there Lorna?" the course male voice called from a distance.

"A new puppy of course," yelled back a young female Scots accent in front of me. I was being led off by a strange girl who I had not even set eyes on.

I couldn't resist myself. It wasn't Master or Mistress, after all. "Where are you taking me?"

The girl stopped so quickly that I piled into the back of her. I felt a hand grip my chin. "I'm taking you to a party, slut," she said.

I felt another hand slide into my blouse and she gave my nipple a cruel pinch. "That's the last time you will speak without permission," I was warned. "Now shut your whore mouth and come on like a good doggy!" She yanked on the lead and I dutifully followed on again.

I was taken along a corridor and through several doors. She pushed me into a sitting position and I realised I was on a toilet. "Piss!" A single command and I did my best to follow it.

Once she was satisfied my bladder was empty, the young woman pulled me to my feet and bent me over at the waist; supporting my upper body on a bench or something. I felt hands on my arse and tried to protest but was silenced with a hard slap across my buttocks. The fingers spread my most secret place wide open and something cold was suddenly squirted inside. The fingers massaged the lube into me and then an object was placed against my little ring piece and popped inside. It was a little uncomfortable but not painful; it wasn't large. Just as I started to get used to the feeling, a sloshing feeling started and I began to experience my first ever enema.

It was an indescribably intense thing. I could feel the water moving around inside me and the pressure inexorably built. As my stomach began to bloat, it pulled on the skin across my lower body and I became very aware of my pussy lips. She filled me as far as I could take and then some more. I was desperate to let it all out but she made me wait. When the hose finally came down and she sat me down on the loo, the relief was like nothing I had ever imagined. It was like a dam breaking; a more satisfying experience than any orgasm I had had before.

I was cleaned up, my skirt was pulled back down and then, to my relief, I felt her unfasten my wrists. "You're ready, my slut," she murmured, as her hands began to explore me. "Let's try you out before they call for you." Her hands squeezed my tits through my blouse and her lips found my mouth. I wanted to resist, I really did. My body relaxed and I submitted to this unknown young woman as her tongue slipped into my mouth and a hand moved up my skirt to find my cunt.

I was lost in her pleasure and time slipped by. She never attempted to undress me but took full advantage of my eager body all the same. My pussy buzzed and my head span. I had no idea just how long I stood there with an unknown girl's fingers in my pussy and lips but it came abruptly to an end when a mobile phone chimed with an incoming message. "Time to go," she announced, whipping her hand out and straightening my clothes.

Lorna, if that was her real name, tugged my lead and I automatically followed. "Uh, not like that," she exclaimed. "Doggies go on all fours." I felt a hand on my shoulder, pushing me to the floor. "Down doggy!"

Once I was on my hands and knees, we moved off again. A door opened and I heard the buzz of conversation. As we walked, the sound got louder, until another door was opened and I was hit by a wall of sound. I was on my hands and knees, with no underwear on and a dog collar around my neck, in the middle of a house party.

"Good doggy," said a strange female voice and a hand patted me on the head. "Look darling, she's adorable. You must fuck her!"

A deep, melodic and I think, black, voice replied. "Of course my darling. I will be at the front of the queue to fuck her brains out when Master Damion makes her available."

"You should have her arse," the unknown woman stroked my cheek. "She can lick my pussy while you sodomise the little slut!"

"If it makes you happy, my cupcake," the man chuckled. The conversation was now soaked up in the background noise as my temporary Mistress led me on. I was fondled, stroked and complimented; always in the third person as an object, a pet.

Finally, we came to a stop again and I heard a familiar voice. "May we present to you our newest pet, Master Damion?"

The new voice sent shivers down my spine. It was masculine, sexy, slightly cruel and full of promise. "She's just right, Louise. Very sweet. Where did you find her?"

"She teaches at my son's school, Sir."

A hand under my chin, lifted my face. "St Theresa's? How interesting! The Headmaster is a good friend. What is she called?"

"Corrie Willoughby."

"I'll remember that." The next question was aimed at me. "Sit up on your haunches my child." A yank on the lead made his instruction clear. I lifted my hands from the floor and knelt up.

"Let me see her," he commanded. There were now hands all over my upper body and I felt my blouse being carefully unbuttoned and pulled off my shoulders.

"Magnifique!" Damion's exclamation made me wonder now if he was French, although he spoke English with a flawless accent. Hands which could only be his weighed my tits and flicked at my nipples. "She is quite the most beautiful object here tonight." I heard the unmistakable sound of a zip unfastening right in front of my face. "Forgive me abusing my position as host, my guests. I wish to be first in sampling this cute little puppy." My nostrils filled with a very masculine smell and a heavy cock bumped against my lips. I instinctively opened my mouth and before I knew it, I was sucking his cock.

I loved to give a blow job but was still getting accustomed to the way a Dom expected to receive it. My arms went behind my back and his hands on my head pulled me on to his shaft. I gagged a little as the fat helmet bumped against my glottis and then I managed to relax enough to take it into my throat as the Master insisted.

Someone was behind me, reaching around to hold my tits. As they got closer, I felt breasts crush against my back and the familiar scent of my Mistress's perfume. She moulded her body against mine and pressed our cheeks together to guide my movements. It seemed as though she didn't want to take any risk of me disappointing this man. I wondered who he was. He must be quite a dominating personality to intimidate such a powerful

Domme as my Mistress. Her embrace was comforting and I focused on her, rather than the cruel cock which was now chafing my throat.

Suddenly my blindfold was whipped off and I blinked in the bright light. I couldn't help but squint up at the man who was ravishing me, even though I knew I might be punished for it. He was something like I expected. Dark, brooding and very, very handsome. I could now hear the noises of sex all around me but could see little but this Master Damion.

Abruptly, he pushed me back and his cock slipped from my lips. "I could very easily finish in those soft lips," he announced, clearly not talking to me. "She should be shared though," he continued. "I must think of my guests." He pulled me to my feet. "I'll finish in your wife," he told Master Mike, as I was led back into the party throng.

Now allowed to use my power of sight again, I could also see the young woman who was leading me around. She was actually nothing like I imagined her. She was younger than me but the lilting Scots accent belonged to a hard bodied black girl, with a skin tone as dark as any I had ever seen. She looked like highly polished ebony. As she pulled me away from the top of the room, I saw Mistress Louise being bent over a table, while the magnificent Dom speared her from behind. I left her moaning behind me as I focused on rest of the room.

I was surprised to see another sex slave, with a doggy collar on just like me. The plump brunette was naked on her hands and knees as an Indian man humped her throat. A dusky maiden, presumably his wife, was behind her and pumping the girl with her fingers in time with her man's strokes. I was led past her and got a good look at her from the front and was shocked to see she wasn't plump at all, she was an over-exaggerated pear-shape. Her backside was big but firm but her body tapered upwards to slim shoulders and little titties. She was really pretty in a sophisticated way; like an Italian cocktail waitress. The young woman looked built for sex and I really found her very beautiful.

I was put next to the other slave and my skirt removed. The Asian man clearly liked the look of me as he promptly swapped her mouth for mine. His cock definitely tasted different to the last one; sort of spicy. I felt a tongue on my arse pucker and hands on my swinging tits. I was, as the man said, being passed around the guests.

I pleasured a lot of men and several women over the course of an hour or so. Oddly though, I was never fucked and neither was Red. I had the feeling we were being saved for something. That didn't seem to restrain the guests though. They were fucking all over the place! While I serviced over a dozen different men, hip to hip with the voluptuous redhead, I saw Mistress Louise with at least four different cocks in her.

"Time for the games!" It was Master Damion, bringing the room to attention. The man in my mouth stepped aside and I looked back up the room to see the low stage I had been first used on now had a bed and some sort of waist-height padded bar, with restraints around it, both hanging from the ceiling and attached to the floor and the apparatus. We were both taken up to the stage and sat down side by side on the bed.

The host continued. "Many of you be will be familiar with this game," he told the room, as he sat between us and rolled one of my nipples between his finger and thumb. "Just for the rest of you... and of course our new pet here, let me explain the rules." I sat, waiting for a lengthy explanation. He lifted my chin in his hand. "You, my darling make her cum as quickly as you can and," he stroked the other girl's cheek gently. "You make *her* cum as fast as you can."

I couldn't help myself. "What does the winner get?" My Mistress looked shocked.

The host dipped his head and sucked my long nipple into his mouth before replying, as he looked deep into my eyes. "Trust me," he said as he stood. "You don't want to lose."

The other girl wasted no time. She scooted across and slid a soft hand up my inner thigh. "I've played this game before," she confided. "I'm very good!"

"You're very beautiful," I told her, stifling a moan as she found my clit. "What's your name?"

"I'm Kim," she said, sliding a finger into my very moist pussy. "You're going to lose!"

I pushed her down on to the bed and kissed her roughly as I fondled her tits. Then, drawn like a bee to honey to her pretty little bosoms, I moved down her body and began to lick on her nipples.

Kim's reaction to my touch was electric. It was almost as though I had slapped her face. Her eyes opened wide, as did her mouth and she couldn't help stifle a moan. I never knew a woman's nipples could be so sensitive and mine certainly weren't. I wondered how far I could take this. Opening my mouth, I gently took a nipple into my mouth and softly nipped it with my teeth. Her hand shot away from my pussy and she groaned out loud. "Ohhhhh!" I had her. Pushing her on to her back, I sucked Kim's nipples for all I was worth as my fingers found her clit.

It was no competition. Kim tried to retake the initiative but her head was as fucked as her pussy. I let her nipple slip from my lips, seized both of her nipples between my fingers and thumbs and pinched hard as I devoured her mouth. Her body jerked and she came hard and loud. "Ohhhhhh fuck!"

The room actually applauded. It was surreal. Master Damion stepped forward and pulled me to my feet. "We have a winner!" Several of the guests pulled a semi-comatose Kim off the bed. "More importantly," the host continued. "We have a loser!" I watched as she was dragged off to the padded bar. She was bent over at the waist, her wrists were fastened to a thick bungee rope that hung from the ceiling; pulling her arms cruelly upwards and then two other bungees were pulled from the floor so cruel looking clips at the end could be attached to the poor girl's nipples. Her little tits were now pulled towards the floor, stretching them to improbable levels and the only way she could relieve the almost unbearable strain in her shoulders was to stretch them even more. "Who's the first couple?" Damion held out a leather flogger.

The two who stepped forward were remarkable to look at. He was a black African; six foot seven of solid muscle and dressed impeccably; apart from the thick, long root jutting from his fly. I had never seen such a cock before and felt my mouth involuntarily watering at the sight of it. The woman on the other hand was almost as tall but a direct contrast otherwise. So blonde and fair, she looked Scandinavian. She was undoubtedly the most beautiful woman in the room and had a killer body. It was she who took the whip. Her husband walked around to Kim's head and roughly grabbed a handful of hair.

I watched with wide eyes for a few moments as Kim's big upturned arse was whipped hard by the statuesque woman and her husband effectively gagged her with his horse-like cock. The Bridget Nielsen double was clearly very strong and she didn't hold back with the flogger. Kim's firm behind turned red almost immediately and soon looked black and blue as her wails of distress were muffled to the level of the background noises of the room.

My attention was then captured by Master Damion. Grabbing my legs, he pulled my hips towards him on the bed and pushed my shoulders down to the mattress. "I get to use the winning pussy first," he told me, pushing my thighs wider apart with his hips as he advanced on me. He was big all right but nowhere near the scale of the black man who was now humping Kim's abused throat. I then forgot about the other girl for a while as my pussy was slowly but surely prised apart by the Dom's shaft of meat.

Damion was a Master of sex! As his wonderful cock slowly wormed its way inside me, he nibbled at my lower lip as his fingers played a symphony across my breasts. I moaned with unsuppressed pleasure as he began to move in me.

For the next ten minutes, I was fucked hard and fast. My breath was ragged in my throat as the host battered my little cunt with his punishing rod. Then he flipped me effortlessly over on to my hands and knees and I got a good view of the action on the whipping bar as he plundered me again.

The bar had been set lower than I realised. I thought it was positioned so that the unfortunate girl's sex was easily available but it wasn't her pussy that was being used. As the tall blonde stood at Kim's head, idly whipping the sides of her small, tortured tits, her husband was stuffing his superhuman sized cock into her tiny arse.

Kim was panting like an exhausted dog or a woman in labour. The black man gripped her securely by her firm buttocks; easing them apart as he used the solid backstop of the bar to skewer the poor young woman.

After what seemed like an eternal stand-off, something finally gave. There was a shift at her arse-end as Kim lifted her head and screamed with a sound that silenced the room for a moment.

My own clitoris grabbed my attention all of a sudden. Damion was slamming into me from behind, faster and harder than I had ever experienced. My body glowed all over with sweat and I had completely lost control of my vocal chords. I was babbling like a mad-woman as my head turned to mush and my whole body twitched with pleasure.

Then it hit, like an Asian tsunami. "Oh my god! Yeeeees!" My whole body shuddered and convulsed as a kaleidoscope exploded in my brain. My Master gripped my hips tightly, moaned and I felt his cock burp wave after wave of thick, hot spunk into my womb. As I struggled to regain some cognitive function, I tried to work out where I was in my cycle to figure out whether this magnificent man had actually impregnated me. The last thing I wanted was a baby but I couldn't stop the thought that I would be incredibly proud for this man, whom I didn't even know, to be the father of my child. I realised that was a bizarre idea even as I thought it.

"You're a good fuck, child," Master Damion told me as he withdrew his sticky cock from me. I wondered at how I had stopped being a responsible adult and become a child in recent days. He kissed me on the forehead and stood, to make room for the next person. "You will entertain all of my guests tonight, little one," he told me as he departed.

The next man took me on my belly and I was able to watch the incredible sight of Kim being buggered by a small Chinese woman with a strap on. Mistress Louise knelt down and stroked my cheek as I was jerked up and down the bed. "You're next on the bar," she told me with a smile.

SEDUCING THE TRAINEE TEACHER
Teacher Sex #4

The school dynamic had changed since Sarah was spanked and then fucked by her head teacher and other assorted members of staff. She was still professional in the classroom, there was no doubt about that. But her pussy was permanently dilated as she constantly thought about where her next fucking was coming from. Her summonses to the Head's office were infrequent but when they happened it was intense and for the rest of the time, she was waiting for the call.

Then Fay arrived. Bright, wide-eyed trainee teacher, Fay!

Knock! Knock! The fresh face appeared around Sarah's classroom door and then the waif-like body. Her pussy tingled at the innocence of the girl. "Er, excuse me. Miss Hadrian? I'm your student for the week, Fay!"

Sarah smiled broadly. "Come in, darling. You don't have to call me *Miss*. You're not that sort of student!"

"Thank you," she smiled gratefully. "Er….?"

"Sarah," the teacher finished the sentence for her as her mind wandered with filthy possibilities for the girl.

And for the next few days, Sarah just sat at the back of the class and watched the nervous young woman follow her lesson plans. She wasn't much more than a girl, the freckles and wide eyes making her look probably even more innocent than she actually was. With each hour of observation, watching every movement of the willowy but awkward girl with her slim arms, flat stomach and pointy little bosoms, Sarah's pussy got more and more moist. She could see no outcome other than jumping the little cutie and humping her brains out at the first opportunity!

Finally, the week rolled to an end, the kids left the classroom to go home for the weekend and Sarah went to the ladies, while Fay started to write up her evaluations. The older woman took one look over her shoulder at the slim little nymph, with her cute spikey hair and succulent body, in the cheeky mini dress she had chosen for her last day, then hurried out. Sarah really did need to pee but she had another need that was far more pressing.

Sarah had her favourite stall in the staff toilet, with a few accessories tucked away in a private place behind the cistern. Sometimes the horny slut got so hot, she needed a good drilling during the school day and this was definitely one of those times. She needed to take the edge off before she ripped Fay's clothes off her nubile young body and, well, girl-raped her! She pulled her soaking wet knickers down and then, as an afterthought, all the way off; pushing them into her hiding place. She released her pee and then leant right back, spread her thighs and gently rubbed her engorged clitty.

"Miss Hadrian. Are you alright in there…?" Fay's anxious voice was accompanied by loud banging on the stall door, that shocked Sarah out of her pre-orgasmic reverie. She instinctively jumped up and threw the door open.

Fay's face was a mixture of emotions and the angry Sarah didn't quite know what to make of her. She looked her up and down, noting her flushed cheeks, parted lips and rock hard nipples. Then the urgency in her groin got the better of her. Stepping forward, she grabbed the girl by the back of the neck and squeezed a ripe tit with her other hand as she thrust her tongue into Fay's open mouth.

"Ugggh!" The young woman struggled a little and protested into Sarah's mouth, but only a little and not for long. After no more than two minutes of intense groping and snogging, the teacher felt her student relax in her hands. She finally stood back and let her talk. "Oh God," Fay gasped. "How did you know… that I like women?"

"I didn't," Sarah smiled. "But *I* like *you!*" She pushed the younger woman up to a counter top and lifted her effortlessly up to sit on the edge, then reached under her dress to work her panties down her thighs as Fay obliged by lifting her bum. "And I like this a lot!" Sarah pressed her hand against Fay's puffy pussy mound and was delighted when her slit pouted open for her finger to slide easily in. "Spread your legs wide, Cupcake," she added. "I'm gonna make you squeal!"

Sarah was lapping at Fay like a mad thing when her legs suddenly clamped closed over her head. "Oh shit," the older woman heard from down below. She prised those strong young legs apart and looked up, straight into the eyes of her pervy headmaster, Mr Pritchard!

"You filthy pair of lesbians," he spat, with faux disgust. Sarah knew him well and had absolutely no doubt about where this was heading. She stood up straight and wiped the cum from her lips as she watched the stage show. He pointed straight at Fay and Sarah saw his eyes were roaming all over the young woman's aroused body. "I hope you realise this is a sackable offence for any teacher," he continued. "And you're not even a teacher yet!" He stepped back and watched as the two adjusted their dress. Fay was absolutely mortified; shock pasted across her face. He gesticulated wildly again: "My office now. Both of you!" And with that final order, he spun on his heel and marched out.

Fay began to tremble and then, all of a sudden, the dam broke and the tears flooded down her cheeks. Sarah took her tenderly into her arms. "Shhhh!" She gently rocked her.

"What am I going to do. I'm finished," the girl sobbed.

Sarah held her at arm's length and kissed her forehead. "Trust me darling, you'll come out of this just fine. Just do exactly what the old bastard says!" Fay looked puzzled but Sarah said no more and just hugged her again.

"Come on," she said finally. "Wash your face and let's go and face the music!"

He kept them standing outside his office for fifteen minutes like a pair of naughty schoolgirls. Every now and then, Fay would start to sob again and Sarah would reach over and surreptitiously squeeze her hand. Which did the trick. Finally, the secretary nodded at them; an evil look in her green eyes. "You can go in now. He's ready for you!"

The Head was sat behind his huge oak desk and ignored them as they entered. They walked forward to stand a few feet in front of it and waited until he finally looked up. He ignored Fay at first and addressed Sarah. "I think you've been warned once too often, Miss Hadrian, haven't you? You know the drill by now though. Do you want to keep your job?

"Yes, Sir," she replied meekly.

"Then you accept my punishment?"

"Yes, Sir!"

"Good," he bellowed. "Remove your underwear and bend over the desk!" Fay looked on with wide eyes as Sarah lifted her dress to reveal her complete lack of underwear, much to Mr Pritchard's amusement and then prostrated herself across the wooden desktop. The Head got up to select a vicious looking cane from a collection in the corner behind him and walked around the desk to speak to the student teacher for the first time. "You, stand against that wall and do not move!" he indicated a good vantage point where Fay was looking straight at her mentor's bare buttocks. "Pay close attention," the Head Teacher continued. "It's your turn next; if you ever want to graduate, that is!" he swished the cane through the air a couple of times and then brought it down, right in the crease between Sarah's buttocks and thighs.

"Arrrgh!" She couldn't help herself. Sarah screamed out loud with the sudden pain and Fay looked for a moment as though she was going to faint. The second blow hit her in exactly the same place and her right leg flicked upwards involuntarily, although she wisely kept both hands glued to the desk. Fay then watched as the sadistic Headmaster gave the older woman another ten, to leave a criss-cross of angry red lines all over her white mounds and tears now running down her cheeks.

"Well done," Mr Pritchard patted her punished behind and gave it a squeeze. "Now you!" He pointed at Fay, who was rooted to the spot.

Still with her skirt rucked up, showing her punished behind, Sarah took Fay's hand and led her back in front of the desk. Pritchard looked her up and down. "You can take your twelve naked," he said without a flicker of emotion. Fay still seemed unable to move, so Sarah lifted her dress over her head for her and exposed her young body to the lecherous old man's hungry gaze as she pulled her knickers down.

Fay was trembling like a leaf as Sarah gently but firmly bent her over the desk in exactly the same position she herself had occupied just a few minutes before. The Head picked up a long leather strap and took up a balanced stance behind her this time, casually stroking her inviting behind. "I don't think this soft skin is ready for the cane yet," he growled. "Hold her in place," he ordered Sarah. The teacher was now standing by the Head's chair and she took a firm grip of Fay's wrists.

Craaaack! The strap made a very satisfying sound as it connected with Fay's bottom and the young woman screamed with the shock of the impact and the sharp, searing pain it suddenly inflicted on her. Sarah smiled reassuringly at her young protégée as she saw the very same emotions she experienced with her first spanking, dance behind Fay's eyes.

The Head stopped after the first blow to squeeze and fondle Fay's firm buttocks again, letting his finger wander into her slit. "My, someone's a bit wet down here," he exclaimed with joy. "Hoping for some cock are we, Miss Brown?"

"N-no, I don't…Arrrgh!" Her protests were cut short by another merciless application of the strap and then another and another in quick succession. Fay's hips swayed from side to side and her legs jerked alternately up and down as she tried vainly to avoid the leather with the very limited freedom of movement she had been permitted. She tugged against Sarah's grip and looked up at her with puppy dog eyes full of tears but to no avail.

Suddenly the strap went down and there was a very ominous but distinct sound of a man's zip opening. Fay's expression went from pathetic to horrified in an instant as he grabbed her slim hips and pushed himself against her. "Please don't let him…" she began to appeal to Sarah but all too late. The older man's heavy cockhead opened up her virgin petals and struck out for her hymen as she let out a doleful moan: "Uuuuuuh!"

Sarah watched carefully but she couldn't be sure of the exact moment of Fay's cherry popping. The whole spectacle was highly erotic all the same though. Once he was fully in, Mr Pritchard fucked the hapless girl like a bull on heat. Sarah released her wrists as there was no longer any need to hold her; Fay was going nowhere. Pinned to the desk by strong hands on her hips and a sturdy rod right up her centre. The teacher sat back in an armchair and watched with her fingers in her own honeypot.

When he came, the Headmaster pumped a good helping of spunk into the girl and pulled straight out to leave her quivering across his desk. "See yourselves out," he said as he zipped back up. "I'll be back on Monday morning." And he just left! Sarah finished herself and dropped on to her knees to eat the cream-pie out of Fay; bringing her to an impressive orgasm and then pulling her back to the armchair for a reassuring cuddle.

"You looked so horny, you made me cum," Sarah said softly after a while as she stroked Fay's hair.

"I never thought I wanted a man, but he did feel good," Fay confided. She was quiet for a while and then thought of something. "Do you think he'll tell my tutor?"

Sarah laughed. "Pritchard! Nah! He's an old perv and this is normal business for him. He's had me dozens of times on that desk!"

"Really?" Fay looked up with wide eyes as she struggled to comprehend this change of circumstances.

"Really," Sarah laughed and spanked her playfully on her bright pink arse. "Now come on! You're coming home with me but there's somewhere I want to take you first." They jumped up and dressed, leaving under the knowing gaze of the school secretary as Sarah led the starry-eyed girl to her car.

They drove for ten minutes and then Sarah pulled in to an unmarked car park. Fay looked across with a quizzical look on her face. "You'll see," was all that the teacher said. The large building had no windows and no signs but it was very obvious what it was as soon as they stepped through the door. A sex shop!

The young woman behind the counter greeted Sarah like an old friend, which amazed Fay as they seemed so different. She was very short and had an enormous pair of breasts that stuck out like barrage balloons. Otherwise, she had black, spikey hair, an impish expression, that was enhanced by black eye-liner, tattoos all over her arms and piercings in her nose, lip and cheek. She was very pretty in a niche sort of way and her looks screamed *lesbian*, as did the way her eyes roamed up and down Fay as soon as she saw her. "Who's your *friend*?" she asked and the way she pronounced the word make it sound like something positively filthy.

Sarah laughed. "She's my newest little pet, Ellie" she confided. "She's into girls but she's just taken her first cock as well, so it all looks good!"

Fay was mortified. "Miss Hadrian," she exclaimed and the other two laughed.

Ellie stepped up to the student and put her hand lightly on the other's cheek in a possessive sort of way that was full of a confidence that shocked Fay. "Girls are the best," the young woman smiled. "But there's nothing wrong with giving the equipment a good work out from time to time by taking a nice juicy cock!"

"Can you sort her out for me," Sarah said. "Something shamefully sexy!"

The big titted shop girl grabbed Fay by the hand and led her towards the bowels of the shop. "Come on," she said gleefully. "Miss Hadrian wants you sorted out!"

When Fay was brought back out, a full twenty minutes later, she had been transformed into a sort of slut schoolgirl fantasy. "Mmmmm!" Sarah grinned. "You know what I like!"

"And you know what I like," the shop girl grinned. "This little sweety knows her way around a pussy!"

"You didn't!" Sarah laughed her head off as she looked at Fay's flushed cheeks and highly embarrassed expression.

"She most certainly did!" Ellie, the shop assistant replied, with a lick of her lips.

Sarah took her time in looking her new plaything up and down, even having her turn around and walk up and down to show off her costume, which the compliant Fay did without any hesitation.

Ellie had done well! The young lesbian looked sweet and demure, like a school girl virgin. Mid-thigh pleated skirt and calf length socks were topped by the ubiquitous white blouse, tied below her perky little bosom. Her hair was in bunches and Fay had been given a lollipop to suck on to complete the image.

"Have a guess what flavour that lolly is," Ellie laughed.

"Er, is it you flavoured?" Sarah laughed. She knew her playful young friend so well.

"Got it in one!" Ellie pushed Fay towards her. "The knickers aren't from the school shop. Check them out!"

Sarah's hand wandered upwards and she was delighted to find a big gash in the lacy fabric. "How convenient!" She buried her fingers in Kay's exposed pussy for a moment and began to explore the hapless girl's cunt once again.

Ellie watched for a moment and then broke them up with a slap on Fay's bruised buttocks. "Come on you two! This is a respectable shop of ill-repute. You'll get us closed down!"

Sarah paid up and hustled her slut back to the car. She started the engine and turned towards her. "Do you need to phone anyone?"

"Why?"

"Because you're mine for the weekend," Sarah grinned. "I don't want someone reporting you AWOL!"

Fay smiled back; a really pretty smile. "I'm in student digs," she said quietly. "No one to miss me!"

Sarah ran her hand right up the girl's inner thigh and Fay shook like a leaf. "You're going to be a changed woman by Monday, darling girl! That I can promise you!" She leant over a little more and kissed her firmly on the lips. "That I can guarantee." She put the car into drive and pulled away.

Craig watched the car pull up from behind the bedroom net curtains. Sarah had texted him from the shop and he wanted a preview of the ripe little morsel she was bringing him this time. This little game of theirs had become a habit but this one was a little different. Normally his girlfriend seduced frustrated housewives and became their first female lover, before preparing them for his big cock. This time, Sarah had told him she wasn't much more than a girl and she was a lesbian. He doubted she would be by time he had finished with her. He stepped back from the window and went over to his monitor to tinker with the settings for the fleet of cameras he had set up around the house, to ensure they were all recording to his hard drive.

Sarah stepped back and let Fay into the house first, following straight on and closing the door. She stopped her with a hand on her arm and pulled her towards her, so they were facing one another and the student teacher had her back to the wall. "Are you ready for this, kitten?" She asked the question kindly, in a soft voice and knowing the poor girl had no idea what was about to come her way.

"I guess so," Fay whispered and smiled the cutest, horniest of smiles that gave her mentor an instant girl-boner. Sarah looked up at where the nearest camera was hidden and smiled. Then she struck!

She moved so fast that Fay didn't know what happened. One minute they were standing, facing one another and the next, she was up against the wall with an impact hard enough to knock the wind out of her lungs. Sarah's athletic body pressed against her and her mouth closed around her own as her hands got busy on her tits and between her legs. She quickly found her moist slit with not one but two fingers and she shoved them inside hard. Fay squealed into the older woman's mouth: "Aiiiieee!" There was no finesse and no sensitivity! Sarah was seducing her like the roughest of men.

Item by item, Fay's new clothes came off around the frenzied activity. There were now three fingers pumping into her tiny vagina and she felt like she was being stretched into a completely new shape. It actually hurt but it was a good pain, as were the teeth nipping at her really sensitive nipples.

She was near to cumming when Sarah pushed her to her knees and pushed her head up her own dress to grind her mound against her mouth; showing considerable apparent frustration. "You're gonna eat me out in a minute but let's get you upstairs first," she moaned. She was pulled back to her feet and Sarah tugged her upstairs and into the main bedroom.

The room was already well-prepared. As well as the hidden cameras, there was a variety of restraints and other objects laid out on and around the bed. Fay's eyes widened at the sight of a bullwhip and riding crop that were standing against the wall. She started to ask the obvious question and protest but Sarah just hustled her on to the bed, on her back. Her wrists were quickly fastened into soft Velcro cuffs and she was soon secured to the bed, with her arms above her head. The teacher ran her finger's down her student's body as she relished the complete freedom to do what she wished with the young woman. "I love the power of pain and Dominance," she revealed, as she pinched Fay's long teats. "How did it feel when the Head spanked you?"

"Ooh!" One of the pinches really hit the spot! "It hurt," Fay pouted.

"And what else?"

"I guess it made me horny!"

Sarah laughed loudly and produced a leather object; a gag of sorts. "This is a ring gag," she told her protégée as she tightened it around Fay's head. "It fulfils a number of purposes, but the main one is muting the noise you will undoubtedly make as I whip your tits. You will no longer able to speak." Fay's eyes widened as her tongue explored the soft silicon ring and Sarah continued her monologue. "Pretty soon," she told her. "You won't be able to stop drooling. Just like an excited doggy!" She selected a flogger with a bunch of soft leather tails at the end. "That's a constant reminder of my power over you. As is THIS!" She brought the whip down hard across the girl's chest and the violent arching of her back revealed the explosion of pain transmitted straight through Fay's nipples. The scream that started deep in the young woman's lungs came out of her distorted mouth as something quite different.

Sarah stood over her helpless slut and laid the tails over those perky little tits, one after the other, as Craig watched the action in high definition, his cock now in hand. This cute young elfin woman really excited him and he couldn't wait to sink his cock into her. She was completely naked to his eyes and the ropes around her wrists and ankles stretched her lean body out to where there was virtually no apparent fat on it at all. She was skinny and small breasted at the best of times but to the hungry man looking down at her vulnerability, the girl looked pre-pubescent. And her reaction to the whip was just sublime.

The whip cast to one side, Sarah had two fingers in Fay's cunt and was wanking her fast; her hand a blur of white when he walked into the bedroom, already as naked as their houseguest. Unable to speak but a virtual slave to her orgasm anyway, her already wide eyes grew wider still at the sight of his throbbing cock. "This is my boyfriend," Sarah said matter-of-factly and completely overlooking the fact that she had had Fay believe she was a single lesbian to that point. "He always shares my girlfriends!"

"How old?" His first question was to his other half, as he was finding it hard to believe she was legal.

Sarah reached down and slid her hand into the girl's open pussy, getting a muffled moan into the gag in response. "Oh, she's legal alright! Quite a prize, isn't she?"

Craig pushed her hand away and tried the size of the girl's opening with his own fat finger. "She's tiny!" He exclaimed. "I'll split her!"

Sarah laughed. "You've had smaller! A woman's body is an amazing thing!" She turned her attention to Kay's little tits and the rock-hard nipples on top of them, flicking one and sucking the other. "You're only the second cock to get in there," she added. "Her first was this afternoon!"

"Pritchard!" Craig grunted. "The dirty old bastard!" He pushed his finger in a little further and began to lightly run the fingers on his other hand over her clit, which got an immediate reaction. "I she a lesbo then?"

Sarah laughed. "She wasn't really anything until today! She thought she liked girls but I think I've opened her mind to see that pleasure can come from anyone. Haven't I sweetheart?" She lovingly stroked Kay's cheek and the girl nodded obediently.

"Did she cum when Pritchard fucked her?" Craig asked casually as he picked up pace with his single finger-fucking.

"Did she!" Sarah laughed. "He had given her a hell of a spanking first of course!"

"Of course!" Craig added a second finger and Kay met out a deep moan around the gag. "Did she get off on that too!"

"She's a natural!"

"We'll explore that too," Craig smiled, pulling his fingers out and unzipping his fly. "She's nice and juicy now. Let's see if she splits!"

Of course she didn't! Kay's love tube was every bit as flexible as the randy couple expected. Sarah had trussed her up with her legs bent at the knee and spread wide, which gave her husband the best possible access. He placed his substantial cock against Kay's little opening, which was now running with juices and pushed gently to get just an inch inside her. She squirmed a little and made some noise around her gag but whether that was protest or desire was unclear. Sarah moved her hand down to the girl's clitty, which was now poking out of its hood and began lightly rubbing it in small circles as her husband eased himself inside of her.

"Christ," Craig moaned. "She really is tight. "This pussy feels amazing!" He was now two or three inches inside the girl, who had started to thrash around the bed as much as the ropes would allow. "You think she's enjoying this or no?"

"Fuuuuuuck!" Kay's eyes nearly popped out of her head. There were still several inches of Craig's shaft outside her and she was sure he had just clattered against her cervix! "Oh God! It's sooo…!"

"Amazing" Sarah laughed and kissed the girl on her forehead. "You have no idea. "Wait to see what else what else we're gonna do to you this weekend."

The horny teacher sat back to watch her husband give her trainee a good hard fucking. It was a horny show and pretty soon her hand wandered across her own body

"Let's ask her," Sarah grinned and reached behind Kay's head to unbuckle the straps and release the gag. She pulled it out and planted a kiss on her slobbery mouth. "How does my man feel inside you, kitten?"

"Oh God, Miss! He's so big!" Kay's eyes were wide and her head was now shaking from side to side as she struggled to handle the big penis that was literally prising her open.

Craig reached down and took hold of her puffy nipples between his fingers and thumbs, pinching them cruelly to divert her attention from the butchery going on below. "I'm pretty big all right, he conceded. "But your twat is fucking tiny! What are you? A doll?"

"She's a sex doll," Sarah said quickly. "And she's all ours!"

Craig had a look of concentration on his face. Then he changed his grip to hold Kay by her delicate shoulders. "She's sexy as fuck. That's for sure!" Then, with a quick wink towards his wife, he slammed his meat all the way into her.

"Fuuuuuuck!" Kay's eyes nearly popped out of her head. There were still several inches of Craig's shaft outside her and she was sure he had just clattered against her cervix! "Oh God! It's sooo…!"

"Amazing" Sarah laughed and kissed the girl on her forehead. "You have no idea. "Wait to see what else what else we're gonna do to you this weekend."

The horny teacher sat back to watch her husband give her trainee a good hard fucking. It was a horny show and pretty soon her hand wandered across her own body.

Craig fucked the innocent young woman for a while that way but soon wanted to try her another way and, nodding to Sarah to quickly replace the gag, he then climbed on to the bed to drop his heavy meat on to her face. With a hand in her hair, he slowly fed his cock to her, before suddenly shoving it to the back of her throat and beyond.

"Now you see the main purpose of the ring gag," Sarah chuckled as she replaced fingers with her mouth and ate young Fay's sweet pussy as her partner used her face for his pleasure.

Craig clearly enjoyed the face-fucking but it wasn't long before he was ready for something more substantial. "Let's get the little slut on her front," he barked, pulling out of her mouth. They rolled her over and put a wedge cushion under her hips to raise her peachy arse up for better access. Then Craig clipped her cuffs together behind her back; where he liked a virgin's hands as he took her anal cherry. He stroked Fay's arse gently and traced the curves. "The old bastard held back this time did he?" he enquired.

"He's a sadistic old twat," Sarah agreed. "But the cane is not a good way to break a young woman in! He used the leather strap on her – my arse got the cane!"

"Hmm, I'll check out those marks later," Craig smiled and chose a thick leather strap. "Let's light her up!" *Craaack!* The supple leather made a delicious sound as it made contact with most of Fay's compact behind. She yelled through her gag but the sound was raw and undecipherable. Craig grinned at Sarah and gave the girl another and then one more. "Getting hot back there?" He called to Fay. "The warmer you are, the more you'll enjoy your buggering!"

By the time he had finished, Fay's arse was literally glowing red all over and the tears were running down her face. Craig placed his palms on her flesh to feel the heat and then began to explore her tiny rose bud with his thumbs; enjoying the way she flinched each time he touched her. "A little sensitive back here, are we?" He squeezed a generous blob of lube into her tight back passage and pressed firmly with a finger, watching her bum hole slowly open to reluctantly swallow the digit.

"Remove her gag for me," Craig told his partner. "I want to hear her!" Sarah unfastened it as his finger began to saw in and out of the clingy orifice and Fay expressed herself with rhythmic sobs and moans that coincided with each penetration. One finger became two and as the pace increased, so did the volume of the moans. Craig kept up the finger-fucking until he felt the rock hard gluteal muscles suddenly relax a little and quickly swapped out, climbing on to the backs of the girl's thighs and locating her sticky hole with the spearhead of his cock.

"Oh God, no," Fay moaned as the brutal reality of her impending ravishment became clear.

"You'll be fine," Craig growled, reaching up to grip her firmly by the back of the neck as he eased his cock into the improbably narrow tube.

"Arrrrrgh! Oh fuck! Oh fuck! Oh fuck!" Fay's breath came in short pants, as though she were in labour.

"Be brave, my gorgeous slut," Sarah cooed, stroking Fay's clitty for her, to help ease her anal deflowering and bring her to an intense and glorious anal climax. She wriggled around so she could snog the girl, who was getting so horny she was desperate to use her tongue on something and Sarah's mouth was an excellent place to start – her pussy would be next! Craig took control of the slut by her hips as he forced his way into her. Fay's moans were already changing and he knew she would be begging for more by time he finished in her.

They had the whole weekend ahead of them and Sarah knew the supposed lesbian would be equally under the control of her master's magnificent cock as her own pussy by time they had finished with her. Their very own student teacher sex toy!

Would you like to be notified of our new releases and top titles?

Sign up for our Erotic Dreams newsletter and get an exclusive and very hot, naughty erotic story completely free with our compliments!

Simply go to www.eroticdreams.sex and fill in the simple sign up form.

ABOUT THE AUTHOR

A suburban mum by day, C J likes to let her hair down at night. Always blessed or cursed with a high sex drive, she is lucky to have a fantastic husband who not only looks after her in every respect but also allows her to research most aspects of her writing. She loves to write about sexy submissive ladies because at heart that's what she is. Her girls are put into often extreme and difficult circumstances by strong men, but men who care about them and ultimately ensure they are cared for.

"I write what I like to read so I expect my audience is mostly women, but to be honest my stuff is so hot, I'm sure I have the odd male fan out there too!" admits C J.

Printed in Great Britain
by Amazon